## "Jules, you owe me a dance."

Amid the other couples, Tanner drew her into his arms on the dance floor. She swallowed hard at the warmth of his body so close to hers and prayed he didn't notice her accelerated heartbeat.

"Relax, darling," he whispered. "I don't bite." She looked up to see his gaze caressing her bare shoulders. *Good gracious,* she thought as her knees weakened. What that man could do with a look!

Trying to stay focused, she changed the subject. "How lucrative is bronc riding?"

"All depends on how good you are."

"And how good are you?"

A spark of fire lit his eyes. "Good, darlin'. Real good."

When the music stopped, so did their dance. Jules felt a twinge of disappointment. "Have a nice evening, darlin'," Tanner said, and walked away.

Tanner O'Brien stirred her curiosity. But this was not the time to let attraction get the better of her. Then why did she find herself searching for him the rest of the night, hoping for another dance?

Dear Reader,

I love small towns. I love big cities, too, and even middle-sized ones. But having lived in a small town during my teen years and a bit beyond, then again as an adult, I can honestly say there's something special about small towns that sets them apart.

When it came time to find a setting for *The Rodeo Rider* and Tanner O'Brien's Rocking O Ranch, the fictional town of Desperation, Oklahoma, was born. Desperation is every small town in America, complete with quirky citizens, tales of the past and love always in bloom. Not only does Jules Vandeveer fall in love with Tanner, but she also falls in love with the town and the people who live there. I hope you'll enjoy visiting Desperation, too.

Throughout 2009 Harlequin American Romance is celebrating American heroes with one book each month in the MEN MADE IN AMERICA miniseries. I'm excited that *The Rodeo Rider* is a part of a series paying tribute to the sexy American male!

MEN MADE IN AMERICA is only part of an even bigger event as Harlequin celebrates its 60th Anniversary. Congratulations to Harlequin, the writers, editors and especially the readers!

Best wishes and happy reading!

*Roxann*

# The Rodeo Rider

### ROXANN DELANEY

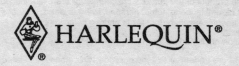

# HARLEQUIN®

TORONTO • NEW YORK • LONDON
AMSTERDAM • PARIS • SYDNEY • HAMBURG
STOCKHOLM • ATHENS • TOKYO • MILAN • MADRID
PRAGUE • WARSAW • BUDAPEST • AUCKLAND

PLEASE RECYCLE · THIS PRODUCT IS RECYCLABLE

Recycling programs
for this product may
not exist in your area.

ISBN-13: 978-0-373-75273-7

THE RODEO RIDER

This edition published by arrangement with Harlequin Books S.A.

® and TM are trademarks of the publisher. Trademarks indicated with ® are registered in the United States Patent and Trademark Office, the Canadian Trade Marks Office and in other countries.

www.eHarlequin.com

**Printed in U.S.A.**

## ABOUT THE AUTHOR

Roxann Delaney doesn't remember a time when she wasn't reading or writing, and she always loved that touch of romance in both. A native Kansan, she's lived on a farm, in a small town, and has returned to live in the city where she was born. Her four daughters and grandchildren keep her busy when she isn't writing, designing Web sites, or planning her high school class reunions. The 1999 Maggie Award winner is excited about being a part of Harlequin American Romance and loves to hear from readers. Contact her at roxann@roxanndelaney.com or visit her Web site, www.roxanndelaney.com.

**Books by Roxann Delaney**

**HARLEQUIN AMERICAN ROMANCE**
1194—FAMILY BY DESIGN

Special thanks to my high school friend
Keith Woods, a real Oklahoma cowboy,
for all his help with rodeo and arena information.
Thank you, too, to all the cowboys and cowgirls who
deal with the rigors and the joys of the rodeo life.

# Chapter One

"I'm not sure this was such a good idea."

Jules Vandeveer didn't realize she had spoken as she stared across the dirt-floored indoor arena of the Agri-Plex. From her front-row seat next to her best friend, she watched the cowboy in the brilliant blue shirt position himself on the back of a horse.

"We can leave if you'd rather not stay," Beth Anders told her.

Jules was tempted, but strengthened her resolve. "No," she said, shaking her head. "No, I need to do this." She knew the dangers involved in any sport involving animals, but running away would not solve her problem. It was time to face her fears, and although she had trouble believing that anyone would be insane enough to make a career of tempting fate on the back of a bucking, twisting animal, she knew her reaction was based on those fears. "We'll stay," she said, determined to see this through.

Beth placed a hand on her arm, concern still in her eyes. "Hang in there. It's nearly over. This could be one of the best bareback bronc rides of the night."

In a matter of seconds, animal and rider burst into the open. The horse bucked, reared and twisted in an attempt to dislodge the man. With one arm waving above his head, the cowboy hung on with the other.

When horse and rider gyrated closer, so did the dirt and dust they stirred up. Jules escaped any particles that threatened to invade her eyes and mouth by bending to reach for her bag under the seat. Over the noise of the crowd, which had now come to its feet around her, she could hear the horn signal the end of the eight-second ride, and she breathed a sigh of relief.

Before she could collect her wits, something struck her bent head and fell to her feet. Afraid to discover what it might be, she dared a glance and saw a black cowboy hat.

"Where did this come from?" She picked up the hat and stared at it as she straightened. Gingerly holding the dusty object, she looked to the arena where the last rider stood waving at the cheering crowd—hatless.

"Hang on to it," Beth said over the din.

Jules stared at her. "*You* hang on to it," she said, shoving the hat at her friend.

Beth pushed it back, shaking her head and grinning from ear to ear. When the shrill sound of a pager pierced the noise of the crowd, Beth grumbled and slipped the beeper from her belt. "I have to answer this call," she explained, standing and scooting past Jules to the aisle. "You stay here, and I'll be right back."

Jules jumped to her feet. "But—"

"It'll only take a minute. Don't move from that spot." With a wave of her hand, Beth pushed her way through the still-cheering crowd and disappeared.

Jules watched her go before turning back to find

herself staring down over the railing into the bluest eyes she'd ever seen, eyes surrounded by thick, black lashes—lashes any woman would kill for.

Her heart stopped and her mind went blank.

"My hat, darlin'."

The comment, uttered in a smooth, slow baritone, caused Jules to blink, but her mind still didn't kick into gear.

Crinkles formed in the deeply tanned skin at the corners of the sapphire eyes. A lock of jet-black hair fell carelessly over black eyebrows. "If you really want it that bad..." he said with an Oklahoma drawl.

Her gaze dropped to the hat gripped in her hands, and her heartbeat kicked in, thudding against her ribs. Had he called her *darlin'?* Stunned into action, she shoved the hat toward him and shook her head.

He gave her a lopsided grin. "You sure?"

She felt her heart somersault before she nodded, still unable to utter a sound. What was happening to her? It wasn't fear that had her heart suddenly racing.

"You okay, darlin'?" His deep voice was filled with concern.

Jules blinked and stiffened at the tingling sensation the sound of his voice sent along her nerve endings. She held the hat out to him with trembling hands. "If you'll just take your hat..."

The cowboy took it from her, his eyes narrowing in a puzzled frown, and placed it on his head. Tipping the brim, which now shadowed half his face, he gave her a tight smile before turning to amble across the arena.

"What did you say to him?"

Jules spun around to see Beth working her way back

through the retreating crowd. She took a deep, calming breath. "Nothing. I gave him his hat."

Her friend reached her and frowned. "Is that all? He looked ticked off to me."

"Of course that's all," Jules said. Adding a good-natured smile, she refused to let her inexplicable reaction to the man intrude on their time together. "You know, Beth, if we weren't such good friends, this cowboy thing would be the last straw," she teased. She nearly laughed at the irony in her choice of words. Since they'd arrived at the Ada, Oklahoma, arena, she'd seen enough straw to choke a herd of buffalo. And she'd thought straw was a staple of the show-jumping world! Rodeos even had that beat.

She'd thought a rodeo would be far different from hunter-jumping, but even the smells and sounds of the evening had brought back more memories than she'd expected. Seeing cowboys thrown from horses had only made it worse, even though Beth had warned her it might. At least no one had been seriously hurt.

"You're sure you're all right?" Beth asked, obviously worried.

"I'm fine. Really." Noticing the crowd had thinned, Jules gathered her things and stood, relieved the evening was over.

Beth took her by the arm, her brown eyes sparkling with anticipation. "Let's get going."

"Where?"

Pulling Jules through the stragglers leaving the stands, Beth said with a wicked grin, "We're going to a party."

Jules smiled. She could handle a little quiet mingling and a glass of wine to clear the dirt from her throat, a place where she could relax and get her heart slowed to a more normal pace. It was obvious she needed this vacation if a cowboy could leave her tongue-tied.

TANNER O'BRIEN spotted the woman he'd seen in the stands with Beth Anders the minute he walked into the noisy bar. Country music played at full volume by a local band assaulted his ears, and multicolored lights flashed in his eyes as a throng of well-wishers and words of congratulations swamped him. And he still couldn't keep his eyes off her. Walking across the wood-plank floor, he felt a friendly whack to his back and wordlessly accepted the praise that accompanied it with a smile and a nod, while someone else pressed a frosty mug of beer into his hand. Rodeoers and fans were one big family, no matter what part of the country.

He thanked, smiled and nodded his way through the boisterous crowd to a familiar face. Pulling up a chair, he straddled it. "Hey, Dusty."

The cowboy sitting across the table shoved his hat back on his head with one finger. "That last ride looked like a piece of cake," Dusty said around the matchstick in his mouth.

"Yeah, sure." Tanner managed a weak smile. His thirty-three-year-old body ached with disagreement. Leaning closer, he kept his voice low. "You haven't seen Shawn, have you?"

Dusty frowned. "Nope, not since your last ride tonight. He was hangin' around behind the chutes and disappeared about the time they announced your win." A quick grin replaced the frown, but the matchstick didn't waver. "That nephew of yours giving you trouble?"

Before Tanner could answer, a female voice purred in his ear, "Will you sign my program?"

Deep cleavage framed by western fringe hit him at eye level, but he ignored the view. Buckle bunnies didn't interest him much anymore. Taking the glossy sheaf and the pen she offered, he scribbled his name and handed it back without bothering to look up into her face.

Dusty laughed when she'd gone. "You've got a way with the ladies, kinda like you do with the broncs."

Tanner shook his head and chuckled. "Bet I'm old enough to be her father."

"Wouldn't have stopped you that long ago."

Tanner took a swallow of beer and considered the statement. "Yeah, but I didn't know any better then."

Unable to stop himself, his gaze swept the room, finally resting on the blonde from the arena. She was a looker, that was for sure.

When the wranglers had pointed her out to him after he'd tossed his Resistol hat into the stands, he'd felt a spark of interest. Old habits were hard to break, and he'd intended to get semi-acquainted with the little lady when he retrieved his hat. And he might have if she hadn't turned up the chill factor. Cold, that was what she was.

"Friend of yours?" Dusty broke into his thoughts.

"No way." And he didn't intend for her to be, either. He wasn't in the mood for a case of frostbite. Without looking at Dusty, he drained the mug, quenching his thirst but not his curiosity.

Dusty tipped his chair back on two legs. "She seems to be a friend of Beth Anders."

"Good for her." Tanner gave in and glanced at the blonde one more time. She sure was easy on the eyes.

Long, golden hair twisted into a fancy braid. And those eyes. Green as prairie grass in the spring. He couldn't stop thinking about them, until he remembered how they'd turned cold and how her voice, when she'd finally spoken, had an icy edge.

When she looked up in his direction, he glanced away, right into the eyes of Beth Anders, who waved him over.

A snort of laughter from across the table cut through the noise of the tavern. "Go do the gentlemanly thing and say howdy to the ladies," Dusty urged.

Tanner groaned, but reluctantly hauled himself to his feet. "Yep, best get it over with. Beth will give me an ear-blistering the next time she comes out to the ranch on a vet call if I don't."

Tanner took his time crossing the crowded room. When he reached the table where the two women sat, he tipped his hat at the pretty brunette. "Evening, Beth," he said, and then managed a brief nod in her friend's direction.

"Hi, Tanner," Beth greeted.

He stayed focused on the vet and avoided the blonde seated across from her. "Where's the professor tonight? That fiancé of yours needs to keep an eye on you."

"Michael called just at the end of your ride. But hey, great ride! Another win! You ought to be well on your way to that gold buckle."

He shrugged. Praise always made him uncomfortable. "I drew a good horse."

"That's what you always say," she said, laughing. "And luck must have had something to do with where that hat of yours landed when you tossed it." She glanced at the blonde and back again.

He caught the hint and risked a look at her friend.

"Yeah," he agreed. The blonde's interest was riveted to the middle of his shirt, the crease of a frown between her high, arched brows.

*Cold. Real cold.* So why did the room feel several degrees warmer?

"Jules, this is Tanner O'Brien, champion bareback rider," Beth said before smiling up at him. "Tanner, meet my oldest and dearest friend, Jules Vandeveer."

"Ma'am." Tanner touched the brim of his hat when the blonde raised her head to acknowledge him. His gaze collided with hers, and his mouth went dry. Damn. She sure had an effect on a man.

"Mr. O'Brien," she said with a nod and the hint of a smile.

He noticed her hesitation when she leaned toward him and offered her hand, but he took it, anyway. A gentleness in her touch caught him off guard. The heady perfume she wore didn't help matters, either, but a man had to breathe, and breathe it in, he did.

"Why don't you sit down, instead of towering over us, Tanner?" Beth suggested.

The sound of her voice brought him back to earth. With unusual reluctance, he released Jules's hand, then lowered himself onto a chair and tried to ignore the pain in his knees. He'd pay for that last ride even more tomorrow.

Beth leaned across the table to speak to him. "Tonight is special for Jules. It's her first rodeo."

"Oh, yeah?" Daring to face the silent blonde, he smiled. "How'd you like it?"

With a quick, uncertain glance at him first, she finally gave him a level look. "It was…interesting."

He didn't miss the coolness in her voice, and his grin faded. "Not much of a rodeo fan, I guess."

He held her gaze, prepared to say more, until she ran her tongue over her lips. His pulse quickened. Lips like those were meant to be kissed. And kissed well. It was all he could do to look away.

"You must love what you do."

It took some effort, but he dragged his gaze back to hers and fought for control. "Love it? Darlin', it's my life. Always has been and always will be." If his body didn't wear out first.

She offered a tentative smile. "I guess everyone has their calling."

"Jules is on vacation," Beth explained.

"How long will you be here?" The question was out of his mouth before he realized it. There was something about her besides her looks that drew him to her. Maybe he'd read her wrong at the arena. She fascinated him, in a strange sort of way.

"About a month," she answered. "Until after Beth's wedding. Why?"

It was easy to see that she needed to relax. Hoping it would begin to thaw her, he decided a little flirting would be harmless. "Well, darlin', I can teach you a lot about rodeo cowboys in a month."

Her eyes widened in surprise for a moment, and then she flashed him a killer smile. "Why, thank you, but no thanks. Cowboys aren't my *thang*."

He stared at her, not sure what to think. That smile had almost given him hope, but he wasn't sure how to take her response. He probably deserved her rejection. She obviously wasn't the type to fall for the line he'd fed her, and he'd made a fool of himself by using it. Not that it mattered. He doubted he would run into her again, and he sure didn't need to get tangled up with her. He had better things to do. He had a ranch to run and National Finals Rodeo to qualify for. His summer would be busy.

Filling the awkward silence that followed, Beth laughed and placed her hand on her friend's arm. "She's a city girl, Tanner. She's not used to cowboys like you."

"You've known each other long?" he asked, focusing on Beth.

"We met in the hospital when we were twelve. I was there with a bad case of poison oak, and she was—"

The blonde shook her head. "We learned we lived near each other and became best friends."

"A city girl, huh?" he asked, as if it surprised him.

Beth nodded. "An attorney, as a matter-of-fact."

"Beth…" her friend began warningly.

"Well, now, I guess that leaves me out. I'm just a simple country boy who doesn't know much about high-falutin city girls, let alone a classy lady lawyer."

He'd meant it as compliment, but it hadn't come out that way. Maybe it had been more of a reminder to himself not to get involved with her or anyone else. But when he stood and looked down at her, their gazes collided.

"So city girls aren't *your* thing," she said. "I guess that makes us even."

As an attorney, she was probably accustomed to winning in a battle of wits, but he wasn't the dumb cowboy she might think he was. She'd thrown down the gauntlet, and he wasn't going to let her win this one. "I guess it does," he replied. "Give me a country girl anytime. One who knows a horse's backside from its front."

Jules smiled, showing white, even teeth, and a dimple. Devastating. Wicked. "Oh, I know the difference," she said.

Her voice was so low it was husky, and it rippled through him to settle well below where it should have.

She was good. It was tempting to stay and continue their duel, but he was afraid he'd say something he'd regret later. "Guess we're even again" was all he said.

She nodded.

Touching his finger to the brim of his hat, he turned to Beth. "Ladies, it's been a real...interesting time."

"You're not leaving, are you?" Beth asked.

He got to his feet. "Afraid I have to. It's a long drive back, and a full day waiting tomorrow."

After they both bid him good night, he almost regretted leaving them. But he quickly reminded himself that he'd have the blonde out of his head before he reached home. She wasn't his type. Her neat, white shirt and pants told him she was definitely out of his league. She looked like money. What would a rough-and-rowdy cowboy like him, who spent half his life on the back of a horse, do with a woman like her?

It didn't take much imagination to answer that question.

JULES WATCHED the cowboy walk away. Wide shoulders stretched the cotton of his shirt tight across his broad back. She could see the muscles move with each step he took. But it was the swagger in his walk that drew her attention to the finest backside she'd ever seen.

"Nice view, isn't it?" Beth asked.

"What?" Jules blinked and turned to stare at her friend.

Beth laughed. "Back to earth, Jules. It's obvious."

Jules suspected it would be wise to ignore the remark. Beth knew her inside out. They'd been friends too long to try to deny an interest. But her little word war with Tanner O'Brien had started her heart pumping, and she couldn't stop herself. "And just what do you mean by that?"

"Oh, just that spark between you two."

"He has a quick mind," Jules replied. "That's all."

"That's all?" Beth echoed, leaning back in her chair. "You keep yourself holed up in that law office too much. You need to get out more. And what's with you, anyway? It's not like you to be so…"

Jules grinned, knowing she had taken advantage of the situation. "Rude? Sorry, but the temptation was too strong."

Her smile faded, and she stared into her drink. She couldn't be attracted to anyone. Not now. There were too many other things she needed to deal with. Her fear of riding was only one of them. She couldn't let a good-looking cowboy distract her.

And Beth would never let her live it down if she knew how that cowboy had pulled at something deep inside her.

When Jules looked up again, hoping she hadn't given herself away, she noted a thoughtful expression on her friend's face.

"I don't think I've ever seen Tanner so…" Beth shrugged and frowned. "He's always a perfect gentleman."

Jules laughed. "Okay, I surrender. He seemed nice, and I shouldn't have goaded him. Chalk it up to too many hours in the courtroom."

Beth was silent for a moment, and then leaned forward. "When are you going to relax and have fun?"

"When I find something relaxing," Jules replied.

"And Tanner and that drawl aren't it?" Beth shook her head and sighed. "Hon, you do have a problem."

Jules forced herself not to search the room for the object of their conversation. The instant she'd looked into those blue eyes at the arena, her blood had felt like warm honey pouring through her veins, slow and golden. She wasn't accustomed to reacting like that to any man. She had never been swayed by anything as simple as cute buns or broad shoulders. Or a sexy drawl accompanied by an equally sexy grin. Even as a girl, she had never been boy-crazy. Horses and hunter-jumping had been her life—until she was twelve years old. When her mount had balked at a jump and everything changed in a blink of the eye. Two weeks in a coma and months of speech therapy had made her look at life differently. Law and the children the law touched were her life now, but she was at a crossroads, even where those were concerned.

"More than you know, Beth. But that's why I'm here. You've always been the one to help me see things more clearly." By the time Beth's wedding was over and her month of vacation was up, Jules hoped to return home feeling renewed.

"I'll do whatever I can," Beth said.

The face of fourteen-year-old Joey Martin drifted into Jules's mind. She blamed herself and the system for what had happened to Joey, and she wanted somehow to make up for it. She just wasn't sure she could. Beth knew that. They had spent an endless amount of time on the phone talking about it.

"To be honest, working on cases in court every day and being a child advocate during my spare time is exhausting. If it wasn't for your wedding and this vacation... I hate to be gone from my work. I know how much I'm needed, but I don't want to burn out. At the rate I've been going, I'm afraid that's what will happen."

"And you insisted we go to a rodeo?" Beth asked. "That can't be relaxing, considering."

"It will be, I hope, if I can come to terms with my fear of riding. I can't help others overcome their fears if I can't get past my own, especially when theirs are so much worse."

Beth didn't comment, just shifted her gaze to Tanner O'Brien.

"Oh, no, Beth," Jules warned, knowing exactly what her friend was thinking. "Don't get any ideas."

Beth turned back. "You're right. I just want to see you happy, that's all. You need to get out and have some fun, meet new...people."

Jules had to laugh. "Now I know why you invited me to Oklahoma when I said I needed a break. Thanks, but I think I'll pass."

"I don't know, Jules," Beth said, looking completely unconvinced. "Like your parents, you've been giving to others for a long time. Maybe it's time to think of yourself."

A bone-weary tiredness swept over Jules. She knew she might be facing a major career decision. Because of Joey, she had become disillusioned. She wasn't sure anymore if she could handle both her career and her volunteer work. She'd hoped that getting away from it would help with a decision and also give her time to work on facing her fear.

"Can we leave now?" she asked, pushing her half-finished drink aside. She hoped they wouldn't run into the cowboy again. When that hat had landed at her feet, something strange had happened. She'd begun to feel things she'd never felt before. Whatever they were, she didn't want to deal with them. She had enough to think about.

And a blue-eyed cowboy to forget.

Beth gathered her purse and stood. "It *is* late, and I don't have the luxury of sleeping in tomorrow. I'm on emergency call until Friday for Doc Waters. With my luck, somebody's dog will chew up a rope and swallow it."

"Dr. Anders," someone called out as they walked toward the door.

"Go on," Beth told Jules. "I'll meet you at the car."

Jules nodded and continued on. Stepping outside into the balmy summer night, she worked her way through the jammed parking lot toward the car. Suddenly, she noticed a certain bronc rider arguing with a teenager who bore a striking resemblance to him. The boy, who looked about fourteen or fifteen, stood with his fists balled on his hips and his chin jutting out. Their voices rose in the darkness, but Jules couldn't make out what they were saying. When Tanner O'Brien reached out, the teenager threw up his hands and backed away. Jules wondered if she should ignore them or see if she could help. Considering what had happened with Joey Martin, although one had nothing to do with the other, minding her own business might be the wisest course.

TANNER FACED Shawn under the bluish lighting in the parking lot. He hated being the bad guy, but the situation with his nephew was getting out of hand. If he didn't find a way to deal with it soon, he'd lose Shawn the same way he'd lost Shawn's daddy.

He drew in a breath of the humid, night air. "You were supposed to get a ride home, Shawn."

The boy crossed his arms and glared at his uncle. "I don't see *you* gettin' in early."

Shawn was right. But it didn't excuse the fourteen-year-old standing in front of him, ready to do battle.

Tanner had promised himself he wouldn't lose his temper, something hard to stick to lately. "I'm an adult, Shawn. That gives me the right to set my own hours. But that's not the point. You told me you had a ride back home after the rodeo. Why are you still here?"

Even Shawn's shrug was antagonistic. "Just hanging out with my friends."

It wasn't so much what Shawn said as it was his attitude that riled Tanner. "And all of them are at least three years older than you. Why don't you hang out with someone your own age?"

With narrowed eyes, Shawn's lip curled in contempt. "They're kids."

*And so are you*, Tanner wanted to say, but he mentally counted to five, instead. "I guess you can't be trusted to get home when you're supposed to. No more rodeos until I see some responsibility." He stood watching the boy, expecting an explosion.

One young shoulder raised and lowered. "Whatever." Shawn dropped his hands to his sides and walked in the opposite direction of Tanner's pickup.

"Get in my truck," Tanner called to him. When the boy didn't slow his steps, Tanner went after him and took hold of his arm.

Shawn spun around. "I'd rather walk," he growled, trying to pull away.

"Excuse me."

Tanner turned at the sound of the soft voice behind him. Jules Vandeveer was standing a few feet away. "This isn't your concern," he replied as politely as he could, and turned back to his nephew.

Her voice, still quiet and calm, reached out in the darkness beyond the lights. "You're right, it isn't, but maybe I can help."

Tanner reluctantly released his nephew, expecting him to take off. Instead, Shawn retreated a few steps and stopped, watching them. Tanner took a deep breath and faced Jules. "I don't know why I should listen to a woman who thinks I'm a horse's—"

"I apologize. Truly," Jules said, cutting him off. "I was very rude, and I'm sorry."

The anger drained from Tanner at the sincerity in her voice, the caring he saw in her eyes, until he reminded himself she was butting in where she didn't belong. "I can handle this."

She drew closer. "I've seen hundreds of kids go through the court system," she said, "and I work with those who have slipped through the cracks. There are better ways to handle problems than arguing. And better places to do it than a tavern parking lot."

"Now, hold on." Tanner planted his feet in the gravel of the lot and stared down into her eyes. "I'm trying to get him into the truck so we can go home. If he'd done what he should have—"

"Try talking to him."

Tanner opened his mouth to tell her he'd been trying

to do exactly that. Instead, he shut it, his anger gone, replaced by something that was close to admiration. She was gutsy enough to stand up to him. But hadn't he realized that earlier?

She laid a hand on his arm, and he felt a warmth go through him like a shot of whiskey before she jerked her hand away. Apparently she'd felt something, too.

"You're upset," she said in that same, smooth voice. "Let me talk to him."

Too busy trying to figure out his reaction to her touch, Tanner nodded. He watched her approach Shawn and heard her lowered voice as she spoke to the boy. Tanner shook his head, amazed to see Shawn nodding at whatever she was saying. Lately, agreement from Shawn was rare. Tanner was even more surprised when his nephew walked to the pickup and got in it without an argument.

"He'll be okay," Jules said when she returned. Her lips curved into a smile. "Try talking to him tomorrow when you're both calmer."

The warmth of her smile muddled his mind. And it wasn't from the one beer he'd shared with Dusty. The woman had an intoxicating effect on him that he couldn't seem to shake.

"What did you say to him?"

She shrugged and glanced toward his pickup, where Shawn waited. "I told him that it's late and we're all tired. Maybe tomorrow would be a better day to discuss things."

"That's it?" he asked.

Her smile was sweet but tired as she nodded, then turned away. He watched her walk to a late-model sedan, knowing he was a fool for letting her distract him. Shawn and qualifying for National Finals Rodeo were his only concerns. But he hadn't counted on meeting a woman like her. He was sorry he probably wouldn't see her again.

## Chapter Two

Jules regarded the opulence of the Grand Ballroom in Oklahoma City's Waterford Hotel, then reached for a glass of champagne from a passing waiter. She turned to Beth. "This is beautiful. I'm glad you invited me. I'm finally beginning to feel like I'm on vacation."

"I wish I weren't so busy," Beth answered with a regretful smile. "As soon as Doc Waters gets back, we can spend more time together and have a real vacation."

"Don't worry about it. Just getting away from everything is good." Taking a sip of her drink, Jules wrinkled her nose at the bubbles and surveyed the crowd. Strains of music from a small orchestra drifted softly throughout the room, while an occasional peal of feminine laughter could be heard above the buzz of conversation. "I didn't know you traveled in such impressive social circles."

Beth tipped her head back and laughed. "Thank Michael for that. Being the soon-to-be-wife of a professor does have its perks. Now that Oklahoma State has opened a campus here in Oklahoma City, things are really happening." Leaning closer to Jules, she lowered her voice. "Everyone is nice, but still, I'm glad you're here to share it with me."

Even though she didn't know anyone, Jules enjoyed watching the people. Jewels sparkled and dresses shimmered. Having grown up in a home considered wealthy, she was aware of the power of money and pleased to know this was a fund-raising event for the local arts council. Her parents, who had always been known for their philanthropy, would be happy to learn she was attending something worthy.

"Where is Michael, anyway?" she asked, still perusing the room.

Beth craned her neck to search. "He's here somewhere." She chuckled and shook her head. "He probably bumped into someone and is deep in conversation, while the two of us stand here like a couple of lost souls."

Seeing a group in obviously expensive, custom-tailored tuxedos, Jules scanned the knot of men for Beth's fiancé. The back of one particular figure caught her attention and she gave a small, involuntary gasp.

"Is something wrong?" Beth asked.

Jules shook her head and silently laughed at herself. Of course it wasn't who she imagined. How ridiculous! But the resemblance was uncanny. Her gaze took in the black hair and traveled down the wide expanse of exquisitely tailored broad shoulders. Lowering her blatant scrutiny, she checked out his shoes. Black, shiny patent leather. Not cowboy boots. Not even close. She breathed a sigh of relief.

"I just thought that man over there was—"

He turned around, causing Jules to swallow a second

gasp. What was Tanner O'Brien doing at an arts council fund-raiser? And looking so magnificent?

Slipping her arm through Beth's, she turned her in the opposite direction and led her away. "Maybe we should look for Michael."

"What's wrong?"

"Wrong?" she asked, doing her best to look and sound innocent. "There's nothing wrong at all. I just think we should find Michael."

"But you said something about a man." Beth started to turn back in the direction they'd come from.

"Oh, yes, well…" Jules steered her through the maze of people in the ballroom. Hoping they'd gone far enough to lose themselves in the crowd, she stopped and took a deep breath, letting it out slowly, while she scolded herself for being so silly. Tanner O'Brien was nothing to be afraid of. She needn't go running off at the mere sight of him like a schoolgirl with a crush.

"Evening, ladies."

Jules swung around at the sound of the smooth drawl and found herself gazing into a pair of ice-blue eyes. Eyes she thought she'd be safe from encountering again so soon, if at all.

Beth thankfully took over. "Why, Tanner, what a surprise! I didn't expect to see you here. I thought you'd be off riding a bronc somewhere."

"Just doing my civic duty." He grinned at Beth, and then his gaze traveled back to Jules, running slowly from her eyes downward.

Jules felt the heat of a blush and hoped it didn't show. Forcing her best smile, she greeted him. "Hello, Mr. O'Brien." Somehow she needed to calm the butterflies he'd set to fluttering in her stomach. His wide grin forced her to do some quick thinking. "I almost didn't recognize you out of uniform. He cleans up real good, doesn't he, Beth?"

Tanner's smile froze on his face, and then he laughed. "Will you excuse us, Beth?" he said, taking Jules by the arm. "This little lady owes me a dance for that remark."

"No, really, I can't—" Jules protested.

Beth was no help. "Of course you can, Jules. You two have a lot in common."

"What's that?" Tanner asked.

"We do?" Jules asked at the same time.

"Tell him about how you help troubled kids, Jules," Beth said. "Oh, and about horses, too. Now go on, you two. I think I've spotted Michael."

Jules silently groaned and let Tanner lead her through the crowd to the other end of the ballroom. Of course Beth *would* locate her fiancé too late to get her out of this predicament. She'd just have to get through it as best she could.

On the dance floor, amid the other couples moving to the music, Tanner drew her into his arms. She swallowed hard at the warmth of his body so close to hers and prayed he didn't notice her accelerated heartbeat.

"Relax, darlin'," he whispered. "I don't bite. Although you do deserve to be bitten for that sharp tongue of yours."

Searching her mind for a retort, Jules found herself without one. Months of speech therapy wouldn't help in this situation, not when her mind had gone completely empty. Even her years of experience before judges weren't helping.

It took her a moment to feel stable enough to reply. "I'd think the Texas two-step would be more your style."

Tanner's chuckle reached down to her toes. "*Texas two-step?* Don't let anybody in this room hear you say that, darlin'. You'd start a lynch mob, and that neck of yours is too pretty for a rope."

She looked up to see his gaze caressing her bare shoulders. *Good gracious,* she thought as her knees weakened. What that man could do with a look!

Gathering her courage, she smiled. "You know what we Kansans say about people in Oklahoma."

"Yep. Dumb Okies," he replied with another toe-tingling chuckle. "Must be why we have so many rich and famous people in the state. But I get the idea that doesn't impress you much."

She dared to meet his gaze. "I know there are things money can't buy."

One black eyebrow lifted. "What hasn't money bought you, darlin'? I'm sure you haven't lived a life without cold, hard cash."

His comment made her uncomfortable. She had seen what not having enough money could do to some people and how those who had it could help. Her parents, for example. But she wasn't willing to discuss it with him.

"How lucrative *is* bronc riding?" she asked, turning the tables on him.

His broad shoulders moved in a shrug under her hand. "All depends on how good you are."

"And how good are you?"

A spark of fire lit his eyes. "Good, darlin'. Real good."

She couldn't read what she saw in his eyes. Was it the gleam of a need for danger? Or was it something else?

"About the other night…" she began.

"Thanks for helping us out." The hard set to his jaw told her he thought she'd interfered when she shouldn't have, but he quickly relaxed. "Tell me a little about what Beth said, how you work with troubled kids."

She wasn't sure this was time or place, but she had opened the door herself almost a week ago after the rodeo. It was worth a try. "I've seen so many children slip through the cracks," she said, "and I feel that most of them can be helped. All it takes is the right person finding something they're passionate about and helping them on their way. Sometimes that means taking them out of their environment and putting them into one that's more beneficial, or helping their own family make the current one better. Most of all they need someone who will listen and give them the compassion and understanding they need."

"That's mighty intuitive of you. How does being a lawyer help?"

She looked up to see him studying her. Taking a deep breath, she let it out with a sigh. "You'd be surprised how often it doesn't, so now I do double duty. In my spare time, I'm what's called a court-appointed child advocate and work with one child at a time, making him or her my total focus, not just the focus of the law."

"Then you're already fully involved in this?"

Nodding, she smiled. "I have been for nearly a year and a half."

When the music stopped, so did their dance. Jules felt a twinge of disappointment when he returned her to Michael and Beth with a friendly, "Have a nice evening, darlin'," and walked away. Tanner O'Brien stirred just enough curiosity for her to hope they'd run into each other again. Not to mention a few other stirrings she tried not to think about. This was not the time to let attraction get the better of her. But she found herself too often searching for him the rest of the evening, to no avail.

JULES LOOKED OUT the window of Beth's Jeep to see Oklahoma City disappear behind them and the open countryside fill the landscape. "Where did you say we're going?"

"I got a call early this morning for some help with a heifer having a breech birth. Not fun, but nothing out of the ordinary."

Jules turned to look at her. "I don't have to watch, do I?"

"Not unless you want to." Beth gave her a quick grin before returning her attention to the road. "I thought you might want to visit a real cattle ranch."

"We do raise cattle in Kansas, Beth. Or have you forgotten? You sound as if I was raised in New York City."

"I don't recall you paying much attention to the farms and ranches around home."

"I spent a lot of time at *your* place when we were kids," Jules reminded her. "I know horses, even if I can't ride anymore, and it's not like I've never seen livestock. I have many memories of the two of us feeding and watering the chickens, gathering eggs and a lot of other things."

Beth's laughter rang out. "Chickens aren't exactly livestock. And I spent more time with you at your house or out having fun."

"And getting into trouble," Jules said, laughing. She had wonderful memories of the times she and Beth had spent together when they were young. Until she'd met Beth, her life had revolved around horses. Then the accident had happened and she'd met Beth. She still remembered their first meeting in the hospital, and even though Beth had been released long before she had, Beth visited nearly every day and encouraged her throughout her therapy.

Jules's eyes stung with tears at the memory. "If it hadn't been for you, I might not have made it."

"You'd have done fine." Beth's smile was soft. "It might have taken a little more time, but sooner or later you'd have come through it. You've always been strong."

"Maybe," Jules answered, uncertain. But whether or not the notion was true, she'd always be grateful for their friendship.

The countryside rolled by, broken only by the occasional farm or ranch. The air was clear and fresh, still cool, but warming with the morning sun. All in all, it was a picture postcard of rural serenity. When they took a turn onto a narrow dirt lane, Jules looked up to read the carved sign above the wooden arch above them. Rocking O.

"Is this a big ranch?" she asked Beth as the Jeep tires spewed dust behind them.

"Not as big as some, but not small, either," Beth answered with a shrug. "Successful, though."

"And they raise cattle?"

Beth's eyes slid to her and back to the road again. "A few horses. I'm sure if you'd like to try—"

"Chickens?" Jules asked.

Beth laughed and brought the Jeep to a stop in front of a sprawling, two-story, white farmhouse. "I'm not sure," she said, switching off the engine. "You can ask Bridey, if you're really interested."

Jules admired the house, with a lawn that resembled green velvet and the many old trees that provided shade in just the right places. A quick glance around the rest of the ranch told her that whoever kept it looking so well did so with love.

A woman she guessed to be in her early sixties emerged from the house and walked toward them. Beth climbed out of the Jeep and reached for her bag behind the seat. "Morning, Bridey," she called.

"Mornin', Beth," the woman greeted her, hurrying to help her with her things. "They're in the barn. They were there most of the night."

Nodding, Beth started to walk away, then snapped her fingers and spun around. "I nearly forgot," she told Bridey with a grin. "Would you mind showing my friend, Jules, around the ranch?"

A beautiful smile lit the woman's round face. "I'd be happy to. You just see what you can do to get that calf out into the world."

If it hadn't been for the woman's smile, Jules would have stayed in the Jeep, but the warmth in it, and in the bright blue eyes, drew her out of the vehicle. "Hello," she said, walking around the hood and offering her hand. "I'm Jules Vandeveer. Beth and I have been friends since we were kids."

The woman wiped her hands on a yellow gingham apron before taking her hand. "Bridey Harcourt. I figure you don't want to go into the barn with Beth for a reason. No harm in that. Can't say I blame you, either."

"This is a lovely ranch," Jules said as Bridey led her

to an area enclosed by a tall, white post and rail fence leading from a matching white barn with green trim.

"My brother built it when he was first married. He's gone now, but his boy has kept it looking nice. Takes some work, though."

"I'm sure it does." Up ahead, Jules noticed a young teen bouncing on the back of a horse inside the fenced area.

"That's my great nephew," Bridey explained, the pride showing on her face. "One of these days he'll win Nationals, just like his uncle will soon."

"Nationals?"

Bridey answered without looking at her, her attention on the boy. "National Finals Rodeo."

Jules watched the youngster bounce a few seconds longer, before he flew in the air and landed with a thud in the dirt. Her heart hit her throat as a gasp escaped her, and she stood frozen, fearing the worst.

"He's all right, miss," the woman said, a twinkle in her eyes. "Getting thrown off Temptation is a daily occurrence for him."

Jules wasn't so sure until she saw him push himself to his knees and stand. She had a better view of him as he brushed himself off, and she was surprised when she recognized him as the teenager who'd been with Tanner. She'd wondered at the time if he had a mother. And if Tanner had a wife. She hadn't mentioned the incident to Beth, so she had no way of knowing. Even after dancing with him, she hadn't asked about a wife, knowing Beth wouldn't have encouraged the dancing if he had. And Beth had definitely encouraged it.

"Shawn, come over here and meet Beth's friend," Bridey called to him.

The boy looked up. Even from the distance, Jules could see the scowl on his face. With obvious reluctance, he walked toward them, a decided swagger in his gait. He stopped just short of the fence and glared at Jules. She knew that posture well, but it didn't bother her. Usually it was nothing more than a cover for shyness.

"Miss Vandeveer, this is my grandnephew, Shawnee O'Brien. Shawn—"

"Yeah, I know her. Uh, Miss Vandeveer, I mean," he muttered.

"Call me Jules," she told him.

He stared at her outstretched hand and then up at her face. The boy certainly resembled his father. Thick, black hair and lashes, tanned skin and blue eyes— though Shawn's eyes were a little grayer than Tanner's. Still, Jules felt sure he had to be one of the most sought-after boys in school. Even his scowl would draw the girls like a magnet.

She looked past him to the horse he'd been riding, which was now trotting placidly around the confined area. "That's a beautiful horse. How long have you been riding?"

"Shawn was practically born on a horse, just like all the men in the family," Bridey answered for him.

Shawn gave Jules a measuring look. "Do you ride?"

Jules had answered the question too many times to count, so it didn't catch her off guard. "I used to, when I was a girl. But nothing quite as wild as that one."

"Temptation isn't wild. He can be gentle." There was no sneer in the boy's voice, no ridicule. "Come on, I'll show you. Climb through the fence."

Jules regarded the horse with trepidation. It did look

gentle at the moment, a far cry from how it had looked when Shawn had been on its back. But she wasn't ready to get close. Not yet. "Maybe another time."

Bridey stepped closer. "Don't be afraid, Miss Vandeveer. That horse loves Shawn. And Shawn won't let anything happen to you."

Jules didn't follow as Shawn approached the horse. She saw the animal's ears go back when he reached out, and then heard the soft nicker when he stroked the horse's head. She wished she could do the same.

"Come on, Miss—Jules," Shawn said in a calm, quiet voice.

Jules heard birds singing in the distance and felt a soft breeze moving past her. The scent of horses and ranch surrounded her. But she couldn't take a step forward. It had been so long ago. She remembered only that her mount had shied at the jump, and she had sailed over his head. Losing two weeks of her life wasn't much, but the struggle to regain her speech had been long and arduous. She longed to take that first step and climb through the fence to touch the animal, but she couldn't. She wasn't ready. Not yet.

WITH THE CALVING over and both cow and calf doing fine, Tanner stepped out of the barn into the yard. After three steps, he stopped. "Well, I'll be damned."

Beth, following him, collided with his back. "Sorry. You just stopped and—"

"Why didn't you tell me you brought her?"

Stepping up beside him, Beth shaded her eyes and looked in the direction he was looking. "To be honest, I forgot. We were busy, remember?"

Tanner looked down at her. "That we were, but all is well, thanks to you."

"And thanks to good Rocking O stock."

From the corral, they heard Shawn saying, "Come on, Jules."

Now Tanner's attention was on the woman who'd been on his mind for more than a week. A woman with green eyes that took his breath away.

"Come on," he said, taking Beth's arm and pulling her along behind him. She stuttered and stammered, but he paid her no heed until she literally dug in her heels.

"No, Tanner. Whatever it is you're thinking, don't. I must have been crazy to bring her here. But I had hoped..."

He turned to look at her and saw the stubborn streak he'd heard about but never seen. "What?" It was clear as day that she had hooking them up in mind. It wasn't the first time someone had put a woman in his way. But why the sudden change of mind?

"She's..." Beth shook her head, scowled and stared at the ground between them. "You don't know her, Tanner." She turned to watch her friend, the scowl turning to a worried frown. "And I'm not so sure I want you to. I never should have introduced you to her." She started for the corral, but Tanner stopped her.

"Wait just a minute." His hand gripped her upper arm. "What's that supposed to mean?"

Beth stared up at him and opened her mouth to speak. She glanced at Jules, who stood at the fence shaking her head. "She's a good person, Tanner," she said in a quiet voice before looking him in the eye. "Not that you aren't, but I know your type. You're a love-'em-and-leave-'em cowboy. A one-night-stand man."

He felt about an inch tall and it made him mad. "Says who?"

Her smile was lopsided. "Everybody. I've heard the tales." Her smile vanished. "Unless you're halfway serious, leave her alone."

"Well, they're old tales," he said between clenched teeth. He'd finished with one-night stands, as few as they were, long ago. And this, coming from a tiny woman not much bigger than the newborn calf she'd just helped birth, was more than he could take. "Hell, I don't know that I even *want* to know her." He clamped his mouth shut and kicked at the dirt.

He couldn't honestly say that he was immune to the blonde's charms. She definitely presented a challenge. And he did love a challenge. If he took it, he wouldn't do any harm to Beth's friend. And that was a big *if.*

Without a saying a word, he walked in the direction of the corral. "I see you like horses, Miss Vandeveer," he called to her.

"I mean it, Tanner." Behind him, Beth's voice held a threatening note. "You and Shawn are good at breaking horses. Don't break Jules."

"Not on your life." He watched Jules turn toward them, looking fine and sassy in a pair of blue jeans that hugged her hips and long legs to perfection. He knew for certain her emerald-green T-shirt matched her eyes. He'd have to remember not to pay any attention to the tempting sight.

"Hello, Mr. O'Brien," she said when he reached the fence to stand beside her. "Your son's a very intelligent and talented young man."

Tanner stared at her. "My *what?*"

"Your son." She looked at Beth, then back at him, her eyes wide.

"Shawn is Tanner's nephew, Jules," Beth said. "His brother's boy."

"Oh. I suppose I should've asked."

Tanner couldn't contain the laughter any longer. "And I guess I'm supposed to have a wife tucked away somewhere."

"I thought… I didn't…"

"It's okay," he told her with a grin. "There are *some* people around here who don't have a high opinion of me." He shot a look at Beth and turned back to Jules. "No reason to be afraid of Temptation there. He looks rowdier than he is, and Shawn keeps a tight rein on him."

"I don't doubt that."

But she didn't look convinced, and that had him wondering. "You don't like horses?"

"Not everyone is horse crazy, Tanner," Beth said quickly. "That may be your area of expertise, but not everyone's."

"It's okay, Beth," Jules said. "As they say, it takes all kinds. He may think I don't know the front of a horse from its backside, but as I've told him, I do. And I'm sure I know more about the finer points of law than Mr. O'Brien does."

Tanner recognized the soft dig and acknowledged it with a smile. "You've got me there, Miss Vandeveer. But we're all open to a little learning, aren't we?"

She hesitated before answering, "Yes, of course."

Something about the way she glanced at Beth told him there was something wrong. She didn't strike him as a woman who was afraid of anything. She could certainly hold her own in a verbal sparring match with him, and he admired that.

"Are you sure you don't want to get to know Temptation, Jules?" Shawn asked, joining them. "Or we could saddle another horse for you."

Her face paled and she shook her head. "Thanks, Shawn, but I'll pass on the riding. I appreciate your offer, though."

"I just thought—"

Beth broke in. "We have another stop, and then some wedding things to do, so Jules and I should be going."

"Thanks for the help, Beth," Tanner said, following the two women to the Jeep. He wondered what it was that neither of them wanted to talk about, but decided it wasn't any of his business. Whatever had Jules Vandeveer scared of horses didn't have anything to do with him. But it didn't mean he wasn't curious about her.

"She's a nice lady," Shawn announced as the two women drove away.

"You like her, huh?" Tanner looked down at the mirror image of his younger brother.

"Yeah, she's all right. She even said she used to ride."

The smile Tanner was feeling disappeared. "She said what?"

"She used to ride," Shawn repeated. "But maybe she thinks I can't handle Temptation. He threw me off while she was watching."

Tanner glanced up to see the dust from the Jeep settle along the road. "If that's what she thinks, she's wrong."

"Yeah, she is."

Shawn's confident smile was enough for Tanner. He couldn't be prouder of the boy and his expertise with horses. "Guess we'd better get some work done," he told his nephew. "Go see what Rowdy has for you to do."

Shawn's mouth turned down in a scowl. "Whatever."

Tanner sighed as he watched the boy walk toward the barn. Just when he thought things might be getting better, they turned sour again. Weary of dealing with it, he started on the day's chores.

But hard work didn't put his problems with Shawn in the background. While he fixed fence, checked the pastures for water and did the dozen other things that came naturally to a rancher, his mind seldom strayed from the teenager. Even the distracting memory of a pair of green eyes lit with fire couldn't chase away his concern.

Supper proved to be a relatively quiet meal, with Shawn still pouting. Aunt Bridey had tried to draw the boy out, but Shawn remained silent. When he'd finished his meal, the boy had flung himself out the door. Knowing it wouldn't do any good to try to talk to him again, Tanner retreated to his office. Ranching required tons of paperwork, from feed schedules to vet reports, and Tanner found them almost relaxing after a day of hard physical labor.

"I see you're at that confounded machine."

Tanner looked up from his computer to see his stocky, bowlegged ranch foreman standing in the doorway of the wood-paneled study. "You ought to learn how to use this thing."

Rowdy Thompson ambled into the room and took a seat on an old leather chair across the desk from Tanner. "Naw, you enjoy it too much. I don't want to weasel in on your fun."

Tanner chuckled and rolled his chair back to prop a

booted foot on the desk. "It helps with the number crunching."

"That's your department," Rowdy answered in his usual gruff way.

Tanner smiled to himself. Rowdy might like people to think he was a dumb old coot, but Tanner knew better. With a degree in animal science, the older man didn't want for smarts. He'd saved the Rocking O plenty of times with his know-how. Tanner often marveled that Rowdy had stayed with them for so long, but he'd learned years before not to look a gift horse in the mouth.

Rowdy took a cigar from the humidor on the desk and bit off the end. "Shawn seems to be getting more crotchety by the day." He struck a match and puffed on the end of the stogie to light it. "Maybe if you'd gone on to the bigger rodeos like you should have, things wouldn't be so bad with him."

The smell of imported cigar drifted through the room as Tanner frowned. "You and I already discussed this. If I'd traipsed all over the country like we'd planned, things would probably be worse. I wouldn't have been here. By keeping to the smaller ones close to home, he's been able to go along with me, and that's what's important."

Rowdy chewed on the cigar, a thoughtful expression on his weathered face. "You're putting your life on hold for a swell-headed kid. You need to be making the PRCA rounds, not dinkin' around with these little dirt rodeos."

Tanner nodded. "That's your opinion, Rowdy, and you're welcome to it. But circuit rodeos aren't little dirt rodeos, and you know it. They count for Professional Rodeo Cowboy's Association. I can make it to Finals either way. But I'm responsible for that boy. I'm his guardian. He's not going to run off at the age of fifteen like his daddy did. Even if it means I have to give up rodeo."

Rowdy replied with a grunt. "Damn foolish thing that would be with your talent. You'll be running this ranch on your own if you do that."

Tanner knew Rowdy wouldn't desert him, no matter what course his life might take. But if his foreman wanted to put in his opinion, Tanner wouldn't argue the point. "Maybe by the time school starts again in the fall, things will have changed for the better."

"We can sure hope so." Rowdy flicked cigar ash into an ashtray and gave Tanner a stern look. "You're not gettin' any younger."

As far as rodeo went, nothing was closer to the truth, Tanner knew, but he forced a grin. "I've got a few years left."

Rowdy grunted before grinding out the cigar and leaving Tanner to his thoughts.

*One more year.* If he could have one more year, maybe he could reach that brass ring—and have a gold Nationals championship buckle to show for it. That and Shawn were what he needed to stay focused on. Not a woman with golden hair and green eyes who had nothing in common with him except a quick mind and a glib tongue.

## Chapter Three

Jules eyed the box the postmistress handed her. "Is it anything that will break?"

From behind the scarred, wooden counter in the quaint post office, the woman shook her head. "It's usually marked 'fragile' if it is. Beth has home delivery of her mail, but her mailbox is small, so we hold the bigger items for her."

"I don't mind picking it up at all," Jules said, taking the box. "Running errands for Beth while she's out on vet calls makes me feel like I'm doing something useful, and it gives me a chance to meet some of the people here in town." She noticed the large, antique clock hanging on the wall behind the woman, who had introduced herself as Betty, and realized it was later than she'd thought. "And speaking of errands, I'd better get them finished. It's been so nice to meet you, Betty."

"Nice meeting you, too. Hope your stay in Desperation is a pleasant one."

Just as Jules turned to leave, the little bell over the door jingled. After visiting his ranch and seeing it wasn't far from town, she shouldn't have been surprised to see Tanner O'Brien walk in, but she wasn't prepared to see him again.

He took one look at her and grinned. "Morning, Jules."

"Hello, Tanner."

"Hello to you, too, Betty," he said, approaching the counter. "How's Jed?"

"Ornery as ever," the postmistress replied, laughing. "You know how he is."

Jules smiled at the friendly banter and had to admit that Tanner O'Brien was a fine example of a good-looking man. Too bad she wasn't in the market for one. Putting him out of her mind was proving to be much harder than she'd thought it would be, but she kept trying by keeping busy helping Beth. That was proving much easier. She was enjoying her vacation and meeting the nice people of Desperation. For a small town, they accepted strangers without question. Or maybe that was Beth's doing. Whichever, she was glad she'd let Beth talk her into coming for a visit.

When she opened the door to leave, the bell overhead announced her departure, and Tanner called to her, "Hang on, Jules, if you have a minute. As soon as Betty puts some postage on this package of Bridey's, I'll walk with you."

Wondering why he wanted her company, but knowing it would be rude to ask or refuse his offer, Jules stepped back into the building and waited for him to finish his business. As she tried not to eavesdrop on his conversation with the postmistress, her gaze took in the wall of small, bronze-fronted lockboxes across the room. The combination fittings of the mailboxes were testimony not only to their age, but their endurance.

"Another care package for the troops?" Betty was asking Tanner.

"You know Aunt Bridey," he replied. "A week doesn't go by that she doesn't send something somewhere."

"Most of us should take a page from her book and do some good deeds ourselves. Tell Bridey thanks for her good heart and for keeping the post office in business."

"Will do." Turning, he strode to where Jules waited and reached around her to turn the knob on the door. "Sorry to keep you waiting."

"It's not a problem." Stepping down onto the sidewalk, Jules tried to forget about the man with her. Instead, she looked up at the bright blue July sky overhead, glad she'd left her car at Beth's little house and opted to walk the few blocks to the small, downtown business area. It was the perfect day for a walk—something she didn't do much of in the city.

In fact, as Tanner moved to walk beside her, she realized she didn't do much of anything in the city. Oh, there was an occasional trip to the symphony, but that was only when a colleague gave her tickets. And once or twice a year, she took in a community theater production. But those were inside activities. She couldn't remember the last time she'd been to the zoo or taken the time to simply enjoy being outdoors. Beth had been right. She kept herself cooped up in her Wichita law office too much.

"Beautiful day," Tanner said, echoing her thoughts.

"It certainly is. I was just thinking how glad I am that I decided to walk."

"So what do you think of our little town?"

Most of the downtown business area was spread out

ahead of them and stretched almost two blocks. Buildings, mostly one-story, some two-story, lined both sides of the street. *Quaint* and *unique* were the words that came to mind, as each connected building had a design and character of its own.

"It's a very nice town. Pretty and charming. But I'm wondering…" She hesitated.

"About what?"

When she turned to smile at him, her knees weakened at the smile he flashed her in return. Shaking off the reaction, she focused on what she was saying, not on the man. "I'm wondering where the name came from. 'Desperation' is a little odd."

"Odder than Monkey's Eyebrow, Arizona?"

"Not quite," she said, laughing.

"How about Hygiene, Colorado?"

Still laughing, she shook her head.

"Yeehaw Junction? Krypton? Mudlick?"

"Okay, you've got me. Those *are* odd. But why Desperation?"

Before he could answer, they were forced to stop when a man and woman stepped out onto the sidewalk from the Chick-a-Lick Café.

"Excuse me," the man said, realizing they had stepped into someone's path, and then recognition lit his eyes. "Hey, Tanner."

"Hello, Cal," Tanner greeted the man, before turning to the woman and touching the brim of his hat. "Wilma. Have you two met Jules Vandeveer, Dr. Beth's friend?"

The woman directed a friendly smile at Jules. "I haven't had the pleasure. I heard Beth had a friend visiting. You'll be at her wedding?"

"Yes," Jules replied. "*In* her wedding, making sure all the arrangements are made, setting it up…" She laughed, thinking of all the things on her list. "The date is quickly approaching and there's so much to do yet."

"That's the way it is with weddings," Wilma said with a knowing nod. "It's good to know Beth has a friend who can help."

"We'll see you Friday?" Cal asked Tanner.

"Wouldn't miss it," he replied.

Cal took his wife's arm. "Wilma's playing bridge this afternoon, so we'd better get going. Don't want her to miss it or be late. Nice to meet you, miss."

When the couple crossed the street, Tanner turned to Jules. "You asked about Desperation."

She nodded, waiting to hear what he had to say.

"Well, the story goes that people began moving into the area during the land rush in the late 1800s, but the town was really settled after oil was found in these parts a few years later. Those were wild times, before Oklahoma became a state. People swarmed here in droves, desperate to find their own little patch of black gold. As it turned out, the pool of oil in this area was only a small one and didn't last very long. Eventually people either left the area, disillusioned, or they stayed and homesteaded."

She thought about it and nodded. " 'Desperation' makes a lot of sense, then."

They walked in silence for a few minutes, until Jules noticed the large building across the street near the end of the first block. She stopped to point at it. "What's that building?"

Tanner stopped, too, and looked to where she indicated. "The old Opera House. It's closed right now, but a committee is working on restoring it."

Admiring the Victorian structure, she turned to look at him. "That's wonderful. What will they use it for?"

He shrugged, his gaze still on the building. "They haven't decided. Maybe several things. A soda shop or ice-cream parlor was suggested, space for a youth center and conference rooms, maybe some small offices." He turned to look at her. "They're taking private donations, if you're interested."

"I just might be." Her parents had taught her that those who have should help the have-nots, whether it was one person, a group or even a town. Because of them, she had always given to worthy causes and had a soft spot for restorations of old buildings and homes.

He watched her for a moment, as if he thought she was joking, but he didn't say anything else until they'd walked on.

"I wanted to talk to you," he began, "because I have a little proposition for you."

She looked up at him, not sure how to react. "Oh, really? And what kind of proposition would that be?"

When he laughed, she knew she hadn't covered her surprise very well. "It's about Shawn," he explained, his laughter gone. "But now that I've mentioned it, I don't think I'm ready to offer it yet."

"Why not?"

He shrugged and glanced down to smile at her, releasing a load of butterflies in her stomach. "No reason," he said. "Maybe the day is too nice to be serious. But I'm sure the right time will come."

Although tempted to insist he tell her what it was,

Jules decided to remain silent. What if it was a proposition she wasn't interested in? What if it was?

"Rain's coming," he said, as if he hadn't piqued her curiosity.

Jules looked up at the clear sky. "It doesn't look like rain. How can you tell?"

"You mean you can't smell it?"

Taking a sniff of the air, she shook her head.

His chuckle came from deep in his chest and seemed to ripple through her body. "Mark my word, we'll have rain within the next day or two."

She thought he was crazy, but she kept her opinion to herself.

"Shawn mentioned that you used to ride."

She suddenly wished she hadn't told Shawn the truth and had made up a story, instead. But either way, it wouldn't keep these men whose lives revolved around horses from thinking she should be on one. And she wasn't ready for that.

"*Used to* being the operative words," she finally replied and waited for more questions. When none came, she was surprised.

"Hey, Tanner!"

Jules turned to see two teenagers hurrying across the street toward them.

"Morning, boys," Tanner greeted them.

The taller of the two appeared to be about sixteen and acknowledged Jules with a nod of his head, then turned to Tanner. "Are you riding this weekend?"

"I wouldn't miss it."

"Great! We don't get to see you much, and we were sure hoping you would be."

The other boy nodded. "Too much work in the summer and too much school the rest of the time."

"Both of those are more important than rodeos," Tanner told them, "but I know what you mean. It's never easy to do the things you have to do, instead of what you want to, but some things can't be ignored. School is one of them."

Both boys nodded, their expressions solemn. "Thanks, Tanner. We'll see you this weekend. You'll know it's us by the whoopin' and hollerin' in the stands."

Tanner chuckled and shook his head as they walked away. Jules was impressed by the way he'd handled the boys. They obviously idolized him, and he'd given them good advice. She suspected they would heed his words much more than they would their parents'.

She hadn't missed how much people in the small town liked him. It was becoming clear he had a good heart. "They certainly think highly of you here in Desperation."

"They keep me going. Doesn't matter to them how good or bad I ride, they're always behind me, cheering me on."

"Has it always been that way?" she asked.

"They're good people. If somebody needs help, there's always someone or a bunch of someones who are there and ready to lend a helping hand, no matter what it is."

She admired the way people in a small town pulled together. She'd never been aware of the same in Wichita, but then, it was a large city and she didn't have a lot of opportunities to socialize. Her career took up the bulk of her time. Why, she didn't even know her neighbors in the apartment building where she lived!

"I'd better get back to the ranch," he said, stopping

in the middle of the sidewalk. "There's work to be done before the shindig on Friday. You'll be there, right?"

She knew he was talking about Desperation's upcoming Fourth of July celebration. Beth and several other women in the community had talked her into helping the next day to set up for the community barbecue on Friday. "I'm looking forward to it."

"The rodeo, too?"

His serious expression told her he wasn't joking, and she wondered if it had anything to do with his proposition. "Well…"

"That's what I figured," he said with a curt nod, his mouth turning down in a frown. "Tell Beth hello for me."

He turned around to walk back the way they'd come, leaving Jules totally baffled. With a sigh of frustration, she continued on her way. She couldn't help it if her heart lodged in her throat every time she saw someone climb on a horse. She suspected it would be even worse to watch Tanner ride again, now that she was getting to know him.

As she continued down the street, she checked the sky again. "Rain," she chuckled, turning the corner onto the street where Beth's little house was. "He must be kidding."

"YOU MIGHT TRY paying more attention to what we're doing," Shawn said.

Tanner looked across the long table he and his nephew were carrying. "I am," he insisted.

"No, you're not." Shawn grinned. "You haven't stopped looking at Jules since we got here."

Tanner started to deny it, but decided it wouldn't do any good. "It's hard not to."

They set the table on the ground in the empty lot

between two buildings, and Shawn reached to unfold the legs on his end. "So why don't you go talk to her?"

"Because I'm working."

"I can set up the table on my own. I'm not a kid."

As far as Tanner was concerned, his nephew wasn't an adult, either, but he didn't mention it. Instead, he glanced at Jules, who was helping Beth with banners he hoped they wouldn't hang, considering the weather that was in store for them all. "I think I'll pass."

The evening was still young, leaving plenty of time until dark to get everything set up for the Fourth of July celebration the next day. Even though it was hot and humid, the people who had gathered in town were smiling as they worked. But Tanner hadn't failed to notice that the air seemed almost to drip with moisture, and he could see the tops of storm clouds, growing and beginning to move over them. He'd been teasing Jules the day before about smelling the approaching rain, but now he could. It wasn't a good sign, and he knew that when the rain came, those banners wouldn't last through the night. All anybody could hope for was that the threatening rain would be gone by morning. Desperation's Fourth of July celebration always drew a big crowd, and he couldn't remember a time that it hadn't been a success.

"You know, Uncle Tanner," Shawn said, dragging him from his thoughts, "you're ten kinds of stubborn."

Chuckling, Tanner gave in to the verbal nudge and left the table setup to Shawn. Walking over to where the women were working, he greeted them. "Sure hope those banners don't get wet."

Jules turned to look at him. "You keep talking about rain, but I haven't seen it yet."

"Have you taken a look at the sky?"

She looked up and her shoulders slumped. "I see what you mean. You were right about the—"

Before she could finish, thunder rumbled and the rain hit, coming down in wet sheets. Everyone scrambled and began running for cover, while Jules and Beth hurried to grab the few banners they'd hung. "And to think we thought it was a good night to walk," Beth said to Jules.

Tanner made room for them under the green-and-white-striped awning of the pharmacy and waved them over. "Don't worry about it, Beth. We'll give you a ride home. We brought Bridey's car, so there's room for two more."

"If the rain doesn't stop soon, we'll take you on up that," Beth said. "Thanks."

Jules didn't look nearly as grateful as Beth did. In fact, she looked downright worried.

"Is it something I said?" Tanner asked, leaning closer.

Shaking her head, Jules held up the wet, drooping banners. "No, not really. I'm concerned that this rain will ruin the celebration."

He wasn't sure whether or not to believe her. Why would she care? This wasn't her hometown. She was only a visitor. But the worry in her eyes told him he was wrong. She was proving that his first impression of her was about as far off as possible.

"They'll dry," he told her, taking a few of the banners from her. "We'll just spread them out overnight."

"I don't know where. Beth's little house is full to the brim right now with wedding preparations."

Her disappointment touched him, and he felt the need to buoy her spirits. "Then we'll put them in the trunk of the car and I'll take them home. There's plenty of room on the big dining table at the ranch."

"But how will we ever get them put up tomorrow?"

"I'll be in early for the rodeo and can do it then."

"Not by yourself, you can't," she pointed out.

"Right," Beth said. "We can meet you here in the morning and get it done. If it isn't still raining, that is."

Tanner leaned out and looked at the clouds above them. "It won't be. I'd lay odds it'll clear up in no time at all."

Jules frowned again, and Tanner suspected it was because of the mention of the rodeo.

"I'll just go find Wanda and let her know we have a Plan B," Jules hurried to say, using the chairwoman of the committee to escape.

"I'll do it," Beth interjected. "There's something else I need to talk to her about, anyway. I'll meet you both back here in a few minutes."

Left alone, neither Jules nor Tanner spoke, while the clouds moved on and the rain stopped. Jules finally broke the silence between them. "Now might be a good time to tell me about that proposition."

Tanner really wasn't in the mood to divulge it. "I've changed my mind. It's off the table."

"When was it *on* the table?"

Even though he knew he shouldn't say anything, he couldn't stop himself. "I get the impression you don't like rodeos, but it wouldn't be the Fourth of July if I didn't compete. I always ride, either here or somewhere else."

"When did I say I didn't like rodeo?"

"You've never said you liked it," he countered.

"I simply…" She shook her head and turned away.

It was a good thing Beth and Bridey caught up with

them, followed by Rowdy and Shawn. With them around, he didn't have to continue the conversation. Whatever burr Jules had under her saddle was making *him* sore. Why the hell did he have to be attracted to a rodeo-hating woman? Of all the females he'd encountered over the years, only *she* caused the feelings he wanted to deny. One, especially, he thought with a silent, disgusted snort as he walked away from all of them.

"Where's the car?" he hollered over his shoulder.

Shawn caught up with him. "Rowdy dropped us off and parked the car. It has to be around here somewhere."

Tanner searched the street. The storm clouds blocked the sun, and the day had turned to twilight. He could see several vehicles lining both sides of the block, where people had begun moving around again, but Bridey's car was nowhere to be found.

Shawn pointed farther away to a lot near the baseball field. "There it is."

Tanner headed in that direction, not caring if the others kept up with him or not. "Rowdy, give me the keys," he called when he reached the car. Angry with himself for being fool enough to let a woman get to him, he muttered a few choice words, not caring if anyone heard him.

Rowdy came up beside him and handed him the keys. "What's got you so all-fired mad?"

"Nothing." He unlocked the door, handed the keys to Shawn and gave him the banners he'd been carrying. "Stow these banners and the ones the women have in the trunk." Climbing into the car, he unlocked the doors and waited while the others packed the banners away and discussed who would sit where. "If we don't get out of here now, we'll be here all night," he grumbled.

The next thing he knew, Jules was beside him on the front bench seat, with Rowdy next to her, while Bridey, Shawn and Beth scrambled into the back. Shawn quietly handed him the keys, and Tanner started the engine. Jules sat in wooden silence. He tried to ignore her, but every place her body touched his, he felt heat. Shoulder. Arm. Her hip and thigh pressed against his. "Give me some room," he growled.

Jules instantly moved away. Muttering again, Tanner slammed the car into drive, flipped on the headlights and stomped the accelerator. They didn't move.

"Hell and damnation," he swore, not caring about the women in the car. "What did you do, Rowdy, park in a mud hole?"

"Weren't any mud when I parked it here," Rowdy replied.

Tanner reached for the door handle and shoved the door with his shoulder, only to be rewarded with pain. "Damn!"

After unlocking the door, he repeated the action and jumped from the car. "Everybody out."

It didn't take long for the vehicle to empty. He walked to the back of the car and studied the situation. Sure enough, the rear tires were sunk deep in the mud. If it hadn't been for his temper, they'd be on their merry way.

"I'll have to push. Shawn, get behind the wheel." Tanner braced his hands on the trunk.

"We'll help," he heard Jules say.

"The hell you will."

Placing herself next to him, she shoved him over with a bump of her hip and gave him a quick but potent glare. "Beth, you get on the other side of him. Rowdy, you watch the tires."

"Jules—"

"Be quiet, Tanner!" she snapped. "It'll be faster this way. We'll have it out before you know it."

She leaned around him to say something to Beth, and he got a view down the front of her top. His mouth went dry at the sight of the curve of her breast.

"Get ready," she said, jerking his attention back to the problem. "Ready?"

Tanner could only nod.

"Okay, Shawn, do it easy."

He heard the engine, and out of the corner of his eye, he saw Jules pushing with all her might, her head down like a ram. Swearing under his breath, he put every ounce of strength he had into pushing the car out of the mud.

In one sudden jerk, the car took off.

"Hold it, Shawn," he shouted, and grabbed at Beth, who scrambled to stay upright beside him. Steadying her, he turned to his other side and saw Jules on her knees, rising from the mud. Unable to move, he watched her pull herself to her feet and look down at her clothes. She had mud stuck from her legs to her chest. Splatters of it speckled her face, and the ends of her long hair were coated with it.

He reached over to brush back a strand of hair, the silkiness of it sliding through his fingers. "I gotta say this." He had to choke back the laughter that threatened to erupt. "You look real good in mud, darlin'."

EVEN IF HE HAD WANTED to, Tanner couldn't have stopped looking for Jules in the crowd the next evening. Not only did it appear that the entire town of Desperation had turned out for the Fourth of July celebration, a good hundred or more from the surrounding towns had, too.

Strings of tiny white lights lined the main street that led to the park at the end of the downtown area. Aglow with thousands of the same lights, the park held the main attractions of the evening and the majority of the partygoers.

"There's Beth and Jules," Shawn said.

Tanner looked in the direction his nephew indicated, but didn't see anyone resembling the duo. His gaze swept through the throng of people heading for the celebration, past two women and back again. He opened his eyes wider and stared. "That can't be Jules!"

When she stopped a few feet in front of him, the brim of a straw cowboy hat shielding her face, he reached out to tip it back with one finger and peer beneath it. "Jules, is that you?"

She smiled and her gaze met his. "Good evening, Tanner."

He jerked his hand away as if he'd touched a hot branding iron. What was he doing? Getting himself wrapped up in a relationship with this woman would be dangerous, but regardless, he was only too aware of her standing an arm's length away. He wanted to touch her, but instead, he moved away, putting more space between them.

"She cleans up real nice, doesn't she, Beth?" he finally said. Her dive in the mud the night before—a situation even she had eventually found the humor in and laughed about—had been the last time he'd seen her. He'd been running late that morning and had only had time to drop off the dried banners before heading for the rodeo grounds.

"Now, Tanner," Beth said, obviously hiding a chuckle.

Jules didn't bother to hide anything and laughed aloud. "It's all right, Beth. I'd say we're even now."

"Are we going to the dance or not?" Shawn demanded.

Beth put a hand on his shoulder. "Of course we are."

"Then let's go." He led the way toward the sounds of a live band, until they finally found a place to stop where they could be part of the celebration. The crowd encircled a makeshift dance floor, where dancers moved in unison to the voice of a nasal-twanged caller, standing on the brilliantly lit gazebo in the park.

"Not bad," Tanner said from directly behind Jules.

The four of them stood and watched the square dance, and after two more numbers, the dancers took a break. The caller and traditional music were replaced by more current country music, and several couples in the crowd began two-stepping around the floor.

When Tanner placed a hand on Jules's shoulder, he felt her jump beneath his touch. He slid his arm around her shoulders and moved her through the crowd of onlookers. "It's time you learned the two-step, darlin'."

She looked up at him as they stepped into a vacant spot in the circle. "Tanner, I don't think—"

"That's right," he said, seeing only indecision and not fear in her green eyes, "don't think. Just do what I tell you."

"I don't even like—"

"You will." As he turned her around to face him, he put his hand on her shoulder near the curve of her neck. "Trust me, darlin'."

She met his gaze and he saw the wariness in her eyes.

Taking her hand in his, he smiled. "It's real simple. Just follow my lead."

She followed and moved with him. "Like this?"

"Yeah, yeah, almost." He moved her hand, placing it on the crook of his arm. "Try it again."

"Tanner," she breathed, her smile wavering, "are you trying to seduce me?"

His own smile stretched to a grin and he chuckled. "Now, darlin', here I am trying to teach you to dance and you accuse me of something like that."

She nodded her head, her answering smile disbelieving. "Uh-huh."

He detected the sarcasm. "Dance," he ordered with a laugh.

Jules complied and shortly had the basics down. He danced her around the makeshift floor once, keeping out of the path of more experienced dancers. With practice, she'd be as good as the others. Next weekend, he'd take her to someplace nice and show her off—"

His step faltered. "Sorry, darlin'," he said automatically.

What was he doing, making plans as if there was going to be some sort of future with her in it? He had the National Finals Rodeo to get to and maybe even win. His future was already planned. Nothing would get in his way. Nothing.

But the woman in his arms wasn't "nothing." If he gave in to this attraction, would she eventually walk away? His past told him she would. How long would it take? And if she did, would it be so bad?

Beth and Michael danced by and offered Jules encouragement. As the song ended and a slow number began, Tanner found that her hat kept him from getting as close as he'd like, so he swept it from her head and wrapped his arms around her waist.

"My hat!"

"Don't you worry about your hat, darlin'. I won't let anything happen to it." He bounced it on her bottom. When she smiled and slipped her arms around his neck, he knew he couldn't walk away from whatever this was, no matter the consequences. He'd deal with them later. Right now, his future was the second thing on his mind, right after how good it felt to hold her.

"About that proposition," he said, his lips against her silky hair.

She pulled back far enough to look up at him. *"Now?"*

He stared down into her green eyes. "It's as good a time as any."

"If you say so."

There was a wariness in her eyes he decided to ignore. Nothing ventured, nothing gained, he reminded himself. "At the fund-raiser, you talked about helping kids, so I thought maybe you might be interested in a trade-off."

"Like what?" The wariness in her eyes increased.

"With Beth busy all day, I was thinking you might be looking for something to keep you busy. Maybe you could come out to the ranch for a few hours. Get some insight into what we can do about Shawn."

Jules immediately shook her head. "No, that's not a good idea."

Not ready to take no for an answer, he kept his voice low. "Hear me out. You'd be doing me a favor. Shawn's been a real handful lately, and he seems to have taken to you. He needs a friend right now—even if it is some cowboy-hating city girl."

"I'm not—"

"It may be just what he needs," Tanner went on, watching the riot of emotions play over her face. "I can't get through to him. He just closes right up. But with you…"

"He's a good kid." But she still appeared undecided.

He had to convince her. For now, she was the only person he knew who might be able to help. Besides, he… No, he wouldn't think of himself. Not right now.

"What kind of trade-off were you thinking of?"

"Oh, I don't know. I'm sure we'll think of something."

"I have a feeling you're thinking of something that has to do with horses."

"It just might."

She shook her head. "Think of something else."

This wasn't the time to argue or to ask what it was about horses and rodeos that she had a problem with. It was time to get her to agree. "Whatever you decide, as long as you say yes."

She looked across the dance floor to where Shawn was talking to Beth's fiancé. "Oh, Tanner, I just don't know. From what I can tell, he's a normal adolescent."

"Maybe. Maybe not. All I'm asking is that you try." If it meant that he would have to beg, he'd do it. Whatever it took to keep Shawn from running off like his daddy had. As nearly everyone in his family had. "Please."

She hesitated for a moment, and then she nodded. "All right, I'll talk to him, see if he'll open up to me."

A flood of relief swept over him. "That's good enough for me."

Later, when the crowd had begun to thin and a soft breeze cooled the night, he walked her home along the tree-lined, quiet streets to Beth's house. At the door, she pulled a key from her pocket.

Behind her, he leaned down close to her ear. "Jules."

He heard her sharp intake of breath as her hand froze at the lock. She turned to look up at him, and he took the key from her. Moving a step closer, he tipped her hat off her head, then placed his hands against the door on either side of her and leaned closer until her lips were no more than an inch from his.

"I've been dreaming of doing this since the first time I laid eyes on you with my hat in your hands," he whispered.

"Doing what?" came out on a delicate sigh.

The sound of laughter drifted from close by.

He pulled away and silently cursed the distraction and then himself. A quick look into her wide eyes told him all he needed to know. "It seems the celebration is over," he said, stepping back. "You'll come out to the ranch tomorrow?"

"Make it Monday morning."

Nodding, he reached for her hat at their feet and placed it on her head. After unlocking the door, he pressed the key into her hand, bid her good night and retreated.

The voices grew louder.

"Evening, Beth, Michael," he said as they passed on the path, lined with fragrant bushes, to the house.

"Leaving already?" Beth asked.

He smiled. "Yep. It's gonna be a long weekend."

## Chapter Four

"Your uncle asked me to speak with you."

Shawn shifted in his chair and met her gaze. "Why?"

Sitting in the sunlit living room at the O'Brien ranch, Jules saw the wariness in Shawn's eyes, along with the stubborn streak she'd seen in the parking lot two weeks before. Both were familiar to her, and she added a smile before answering, "I don't know if your uncle told you, but I'm an attorney."

"Oh, yeah?" His smile was almost a smirk, but not quite. "I knew you were smart."

She felt the warmth of a blush and laughed to cover her embarrassment. "Yes, well, that's not the point, but I can tell you that I studied a long time before I passed the bar. When I was about twelve, I saw how hard things were for some kids. I was lucky. I had parents who loved me and were able to provide me with the best, but it isn't like that for many. I decided then that I'd find a way to help those who weren't as fortunate as I was, so a few years later, I decided to become a lawyer and help that way. Now I work in the juvenile court, helping kids who've gotten into trouble or whose families aren't able to take care of them."

Shawn shrugged, but looked a bit uncomfortable. "I'm not in trouble, and I have a family. Uncle Tanner, Aunt Bridey, Rowdy. They're my family."

Although Jules had briefly met Rowdy while decorating for the Fourth of July celebration, she didn't know his relationship to the family, only that he lived and worked on the ranch.

"Yes, and it's clear they all care about you," she replied, making a mental note to ask Tanner about Rowdy.

A sullen expression appeared on his face. "Sometimes."

"Only sometimes?"

Another shrug, and he looked away.

It was clear from his body language that this wasn't easy for him, but she hadn't expected it to be. Boys tended to close themselves off and pretend everything was okay. Girls were sometimes easier to talk to, but most children and teens who were dealing with emotional issues tended to keep them locked inside. It had taken her months of patience and trial-and-error to get Joey Martin to open up to her, and she hoped it wouldn't be the same with Shawn.

"Like when?" she asked.

"When I want to compete."

Instead of answering, she waited for him to explain.

"You know, in a rodeo," he said. "Uncle Tanner says school comes first, but school isn't going to do me any good on the circuit." He looked her square in the eye, as if waiting for her to side with his uncle.

"You don't think school is important?"

"Well, sure, but other guys do both."

"Other boys your age?"

"Yeah, some I go to school with. And others who…" He broke eye contact. "Who aren't in school."

"They dropped out?" When he nodded, she began to see the situation a little more clearly and understood why Tanner might be concerned. "Is that what you want to do?"

His shoulders went up and down a third time. "I don't know."

She had lost count of how many times she had seen children shrug, no matter their age or gender. With some, it was a sign they weren't willing to talk. With others, it meant they didn't know how to communicate their feelings. And the sharing of feelings with those who wanted to help was vitally important.

"So tell me about the ones who are in school," she said, hoping to open the door to some real communication. "How do they manage to compete in rodeos during the school term?"

"They belong to NHSRA." He looked at her and smiled, obviously knowing she didn't understand what he was talking about. "National High School Rodeo Association."

"I wasn't aware there was such a thing," she admitted. "Tell me about it."

Shawn explained that it was an international organization for young men and women in high school who participated in or were interested in rodeo competition. He also told her that attending school was mandatory and members must keep passing grades in four subjects. Desperation High School also had a rodeo club, of which he was a member, but hadn't attended meetings since before Christmas.

"Why not?" she asked.

"It's kid stuff," he said with yet another shrug.

Jules laughed softly. "I hope being in a club isn't kid stuff, because I belong to several. We call them organizations, but it's the same thing, where people who share a common interest or career get together. Isn't your rodeo club like that?"

"Well, yeah," he admitted.

"Aren't the other members active in rodeo?"

"Sure they are, it's just—" he shook his head "—I don't know. I don't hang around with the bunch at school. Uncle Tanner doesn't like my other friends because they're older than me. And, well, he's afraid I'll be like my dad and run away to travel the rodeo circuit." He leaned forward, his blue-gray eyes bright with passion. "But when I ask him about my dad, he doesn't say much. And there's stuff I want to know, but I know he won't tell me."

Jules was surprised. Tanner didn't strike her as the type who wouldn't answer his nephew's questions, and answer them honestly. Not when he was so concerned about him. "He's refused to answer something?"

"No," Shawn said, shaking his head furiously. "But I just know he won't."

"Why do you think he won't?"

"I…" He ducked his head, hiding his face. "I just do."

Jules saw a classic teenager, unable to know how to ask and afraid if he did, the answers might not be something he would like or might turn his world upside down. She didn't know what had happened with Shawn's parents or why he wasn't with them. But whatever it was, she didn't think Tanner would keep that information from Shawn, especially if he was asked directly.

Sensing that Tanner wasn't the complete problem, there was only one thing she could do. "Would you like me to talk to him?"

Shawn looked up at her, and she could see the battle raging within him. He was scared, she understood that. It wasn't easy being a kid, especially those years from ten or twelve to as far as eighteen and sometimes longer. Shawn fit in the middle of those ages. How long had he been afraid of asking questions he had every right to have answered?

Reaching out, she placed her hand on one of his as he gripped the tops of his knees. "I think you should ask whatever it is you want to know."

He shook his head. "I don't think…"

She offered him what she hoped was an encouraging smile and leaned back in her chair again. "You won't know until you try it. Believe me, Shawn, it won't hurt nearly as much as you think it will. The anticipation is worse than the actual deed."

If only she could convince *herself* of that, she thought. She badly needed to get over her fear of riding, but every time she imagined herself climbing on the back of a horse, she relived the fall she'd taken when she was twelve. That was her anticipation.

"Maybe," Shawn said. "Maybe I'll talk to him."

Feeling she had done all she could for one day—and perhaps much longer, if everything went as she hoped it would—she stood. "I think you may be able to work out your differences about rodeo, too."

He looked up, his eyes wide. "Really?"

"Well, in time. But this is a first step, and you're the one initiating it. That alone will show your uncle that you're growing up and that the two of you can begin to really talk about rodeo."

Nodding, he finally smiled. "Thanks, Jules."

"That's why I'm here," she said, half joking as she walked to the door. Opening it, she had to cover her soft gasp. Tanner waited on the other side. Had he been listening?

TANNER SAW Jules's eyes narrow in suspicion and did some quick thinking. "How'd it go?"

Instead of answering, she pressed a finger to her lips. Closing the door behind her, she stepped farther into the hallway. "You were listening?" she asked in a hushed voice and glanced toward the door.

"Only for a minute," he said, aware of how guilty he sounded. "He's my nephew. I want to know what's going on. I'm concerned."

"Spying is never a good idea." She turned and walked away, and he followed, until she stopped and faced him again. "Is there somewhere we can talk privately?"

"Sure." He knew he probably looked surprised, but he shouldn't have. There was no telling what she'd learned from talking to Shawn. He just hoped the news was good, and he wouldn't have to worry about his nephew anymore.

As he started for the ranch office at the rear of the house, he realized it might not be the most private. Motioning for her to follow him, he led her outside. There was a better place where they could talk.

"I'm not keeping you from anything, am I?" she asked as they walked across the drive to the barn.

"Not a thing. Rowdy handles a lot of the ranch work."

"Rowdy?"

"Rowdy Thompson, our ranch foreman. He's been with the family since I was a kid. Knows more about cattle ranching than anybody."

They reached the barn and he opened one of the big double doors, letting her pass inside in front of him. She stopped for a moment after stepping out of the bright sunshine and into the dimmer building. "There's a small office down there," he said, pointing to the end of the aisle between the two rows of stalls. "We don't use it much, so there shouldn't be any interruptions."

Nodding, she started in the direction of the office, but she stopped suddenly at the sound of a horse whinnying.

"It's just one of the horses," he said, wondering why she was surprised by it. "This is a ranch, remember?"

Her laugh held a touch of nervousness, but she continued on. "Of course it is. I wasn't thinking about that, though, just Shawn and our conversation."

Reaching the door to the small room, he opened it and decided not to needle her about her reaction. He'd think about it later. Right now, Shawn was uppermost in his mind. "It's a little dirty," he warned her.

"I don't mind."

"Have a seat." He indicated an empty chair by the old, scarred desk, then pulled another chair from the corner for himself.

She settled on the chair and waited for him to do the same. When he had, the first thing she did was smile. "Just so you know, Shawn isn't any different from any boy his age. And in case you don't remember, fifteen is a hard age to be."

"He won't be fifteen until November," Tanner

pointed out. "But I guess that doesn't make a whole lot of difference."

She shook her head and laughed softly. "No, not a lot. Like most his age, he's eager to grow up, but he simply isn't emotionally mature enough to be an adult. Basically, he probably needs you as much, if not more, than he ever has."

Remembering Tucker, his brother and Shawn's daddy, Tanner was aware of that. "I understand. I just don't know how to handle it. Or him, obviously."

"It's a difficult time for everyone," she agreed. "I probably deal with more teens than the younger ones because they have so many things going on inside. They're pulled in a lot of different directions. Parents, peers, their own individual wants and needs… And they don't know how to communicate with others, especially adults. They aren't always truthful with their friends, either, so don't feel too left out."

"I do try to talk to him," he said, thinking of all the times his nephew had turned sullen when he did.

"Let him pick the time. Be available. Don't judge, just listen. That would be a good start."

Tanner trusted her suggestions and knew he hadn't been doing those things. When he talked to Shawn, it was often after he'd let things go too far, and even though he tried not to do anything in anger, it was sometimes anger that drove him to speak up. "I'll keep that in mind. I admit I have a lot to learn."

"Everyone does, so don't feel alone." She leaned toward him, her expression earnest. "You've done a good job. Too many parents and guardians don't even try."

"I feel a 'but' coming on," he said.

Leaning back again, she nodded. "He has questions."

Her face was a mask, giving away nothing, and he had a feeling this was more serious than he'd imagined. "Questions about what?"

"His parents."

The air in his lungs seemed to vanish, and the room grew smaller. The subject of Shawn's parents was difficult to explain. He wasn't sure how to approach it with his nephew, so he hadn't done it. In fact, he'd avoided it. "What about it?" he asked, feeling defensive. "His family loves him."

"I don't doubt that," she said, "and I don't know what he wants to know. He wasn't specific. But I can tell you that he feels you won't answer whatever it is he needs to ask."

"I've never refused to answer anything," Tanner said. "I've always answered, and I know Bridey has, too. But we aren't the kind of people who dwell on the past. We move forward."

Jules was quiet for a moment, as if considering what he said. "Nobody should dwell on the past, but you have to agree that our past is what shapes us into who we are today."

"Well, sure," he said, shrugging. His own experiences had made him wary of commitment. He admitted it and lived his life accordingly. "I just don't want Shawn getting bogged down in all the stuff he didn't have any control over and forget about what he has now. The way he's been lately, I can see that happening."

"He'll learn about the past at some point, and it might not be the way you want him to learn it or from the best person."

Nodding, he mulled that over. "And I suppose it would be better to hear it from me than from a stranger. You're right, that could happen."

"Sometimes the truth isn't easy to hear, but in the long run, it's better to know than to learn at the wrong time and from the wrong person, who may not know the important things."

"So you think I should just sit him down and tell him everything?"

She smiled and tilted her head to one side. "Not necessarily. I think he'll come to you with the questions he has. Maybe not all at one time, but little by little, especially because he doesn't know if you'll be willing to be honest with him."

Tanner jerked his head up at the last few words. "He doesn't? Now that's wrong. I've always been honest with him, and I've been there for him every day since his mother left. It's just that over the past six months or so, I haven't been able to reach him when he's needed it the most."

"I hope this will make things easier for both of you."

"Not easy," he said, imagining the conversation and Shawn's reaction. "But just knowing what the problem is makes it easier, in a way. Thank you."

Standing, she offered him her hand and he took it. "I'm glad I could help."

He didn't want to let go of her hand. She could have easily refused to help or told him to go elsewhere—like to blazes—when he had asked for her help. Instead, she'd agreed, even without an explanation. "Don't leave yet. You don't know it all. I owe you that much," he said, releasing her.

Hesitating, she settled in the chair again. "It would help me if I knew more, especially about Shawn's parents."

He leaned against the edge of the desk. "I guess it would. But I'll warn you, it's not a very pretty story. It could have been worse, though. That's what I've always told myself."

"You have no idea just how bad things are for some."

Nodding, he wondered how to start. *Where* to start. Sifting through fourteen years of memories, he decided. "I've been responsible for Shawn since the day he was dumped on my doorstep more than fourteen years ago. My brother, Tucker, left home when he was fifteen. He was rodeo-crazy. Not that most everyone in this family isn't," he added when he saw her expression. "Shawn's mother couldn't have been more than seventeen when she stood on the porch that evening with a six-month-old baby in her arms. I can still hear her saying, 'I can't take care of him no more. He's Tucker's boy. And from what Tuck said, you'd do right by him.'"

"Oh, goodness!"

Tanner tried for a smile. "I was thinking something a little stronger at the time. Before I had a chance to realize what was happening or ask about Tucker's whereabouts, she handed me the bundle and disappeared. I become a substitute dad to my six-month-old nephew. If it hadn't been for Aunt Bridey, I figure the poor little guy never would have made it through those first few years."

"How much of this does Shawn know?"

"Only that his mother left him with us."

"And his father? Where is he?"

Tanner stared down at his hands, resting on his thighs.

"I don't know. We haven't heard from him since the day he left. So, you see, I don't have a lot of answers."

"Have you tried to find him?"

"Every chance I've had. He must have left rodeo, because no one has seen him for years. If he's even still…" He shook his head, unable to finish. Taking a deep breath, he let it out. "Shawn's a natural-born bronc rider. He's got potential, real potential. With a little self-discipline, he could be a champion a few years down the road." If only he could put a stop to the boy's wild streak. The way things were going, that would take a small miracle. He looked at the woman across from him. Was Jules the small miracle they needed?

"But you were so young. Why did you take on raising a baby?" she asked.

"I didn't know anything about his mother and when I learned later, I wasn't willing to give him back to her. I was more concerned with finding my brother."

"But still…"

"Family take care of their own."

"Tanner…"

"I know what you're going to say." He leaned forward, meeting her gaze. "I was of age. My lawyer and the court agreed I should have custody, partly because Bridey was here to help."

Jules nodded. "What about Shawn and rodeo? As I understand it, you don't want him competing."

"That's not it. He's a member of NHSRA, but he's been lax with his schoolwork. His grades have slipped. He's been hanging around with some older boys, who aren't in school and aren't good role models, and that worries me. When he gets his grades back up where they should be—and he's a smart kid, so he can do it—he can compete again. Those aren't only my rules. They're the rules of NHSRA."

"He told me about that. But I think you need to tell him what you just told me about his mother and how he came to live with you. All of it. Let him know you've tried to find your brother. He needs to hear it."

Tanner stood, pulled off his hat and raked his hand through his hair. "All I can do is tell him what I know. If you think it will help."

Jules stood, too, and placed her hand on his arm. The warmth of the contact and of her smile made his insides melt, and it was all he could do not to touch her. "I *know* it will help," she said. "I'll be around until after Beth's wedding if either of you need someone to talk to about it."

"Thanks," he said, the word sounding like a bull-frog's croak. He was relieved when she dropped her hand and turned to leave. He wasn't accustomed to the feelings she aroused in him. He didn't know what to do about them, and he didn't know if he even *wanted* to do anything.

But there was still one thing he could do and needed to do. He'd offered her a proposition, and she'd upheld her end of it. Now he needed to do the same.

"Before you go…" he said, bringing her to a halt. She turned to look at him, her hand on the iron door handle, a question in her eyes and one eyebrow raised. "Come back on Friday. I'll have Bridey fix up some-thing special for supper, and I'll fulfill my part of the proposition."

He was surprised she didn't put up a fuss about it and

insist he tell her, but he was pleased, too. "Late afternoon? Three or four?"

"I think I can work that in," she said with a wide smile, and then she was gone.

He thought about the night of the Fourth of July celebration, when he had almost kissed her. A part of him wished they hadn't been interrupted, but another part told him it had been a good thing that Beth and Michael had chosen that moment to return home. He didn't know where he was going where Jules was concerned. He only knew she was different from any other woman he'd ever met. Cool on the outside, caring on the inside. A walking contradiction, and an intriguing one, too. Maybe he'd learn more on Friday.

JULES ARRIVED at the Rocking O ranch on Friday at three-thirty. She reasoned that Tanner had said between three and four, so three-thirty seemed like a good compromise. She valued promptness, one more good habit her parents had instilled in her.

She also liked people to be perfectly clear about their intentions, but she had no idea what Tanner was planning. Suspecting Bridey was an excellent cook, she looked forward to being a dinner guest. And she hoped to have the chance to visit the horses, so much so that she'd dressed in jeans and a T-shirt. Now that she knew they were kept in the barn where she and Tanner had talked, she wouldn't be as jumpy. She'd thought about it and decided that this might be her best chance to take that first step in overcoming her fear of riding.

"Jules, come see the new foal!" Shawn shouted to

her as soon as she parked her car and opened the door to climb out.

After closing the car door behind her, she walked toward him. "A filly?"

He nodded as she caught up with him near the white barn. "Yes, and she's going to be a beauty. Come see for yourself."

Following him into the barn, she spied Tanner farther down the aisle leaning over the door to a stall. She hated to acknowledge the way her heart skipped faster at the sight of him, but denying it would be foolish. It was something she would have to deal with.

"*Thought* I heard a car drive up," Tanner said in greeting. "What do you think of the new addition?"

Jules stopped beside him and peered over the chest-high wooden barrier. "Oh, she's beautiful! You were right, Shawn. What a lovely color, too. Chestnuts have always been among my favorites."

"So you do know a bit about horses," Tanner said.

"Some." She prepared herself to dodge questions and was grateful when someone at the door of the barn shouted Shawn's name.

Shawn groaned. "Figures."

A stocky older man, with a definite bow in his legs, walked toward them. "You got one more chore, boy," he said to Shawn. "After that one's done, you're free to chitchat with the lady here, but not before."

Jules heard Tanner's quiet chuckle. "You should've known he'd come after you, Shawn," he said in a low voice to his nephew. When the man reached them and stopped, his balled fists on his hips and a glare for Shawn, Tanner stepped forward. "Jules, I'd like you to meet Rowdy Thompson, our ranch foreman and a perennial thorn in Shawn's side. Rowdy, this is Jules Vandeveer, Beth Anders's friend from Kansas."

Rowdy raised a hand to touch a finger to the brim of his hat, but barely met her eyes. "Nice to meet you, ma'am. Now if you'll excuse our young friend…"

"Go on, Shawn," she told him. "I'll be here for a while. At least until after dinner." Expecting Rowdy to be pleased with her encouragement, she was surprised to see him glower at her. And then she realized she had used the term *dinner*, instead of the less formal *supper*. "I can't wait to see what special supper Bridey is fixing," she added, hoping to redeem herself in Rowdy's eyes, at least.

Rowdy's response was a grunt as he turned and started for the door. Shawn followed with a wistful backward glance at his uncle.

"We'll wait for you, Shawn," Tanner called after him. Turning to Jules, he shrugged. "He was excited that you were going to be here. Why don't I show you around while he finishes watering the cattle?"

With a smile she didn't feel, she followed him, wishing she hadn't been the cause of a problem, but it had been Shawn's responsibility, and there was nothing she could do. "How many horses do you have?" she asked as he led her outside.

"Nine, last count. The new filly makes ten."

"That's quite a few. All quarter horses?"

He nodded and pointed out a group of the animals in a nearby pasture. "We've done some breeding for cutting and rodeo, both. Good horses bring good money where cowboys are concerned."

"I'm aware that quarter horses are the staple of

ranching. I'm more familiar with Thoroughbreds and warmbloods, but a horse is a horse, and you have some real beauties."

When she looked up, he was studying her closely. "Then you do know quite a lot about horses," he said. "Tall horses, both breeds. About sixteen hands?"

Jules realized she'd said too much, piqued his curiosity. There was no way out of it now, but there was only so much she would tell him. "Some are smaller," she went on as if the subject was nothing, "but on average, most of those used for jumping are at least fourteen, but sixteen is better."

"Jumping?" His smile was wide, as if he'd discovered a treasure. "Taller can jump higher?"

She was relieved when he didn't ask how she knew and was able to laugh at his assumption. "No higher than shorter horses, really, but when you're ten or twelve years old, those jumps don't look nearly as high if you're on a tall horse."

"I've never looked at it that way, but I see what you mean."

Feeling even more relieved, she relaxed—until she saw Shawn leading three horses from the other side of the barn, all of them in full western gear and ready to ride. Apprehension slithered up her spine.

"I guess you've figured out my part of the proposition," Tanner said to her as Shawn approached.

Speechless, Jules had to force herself to speak. "Yes, I see, but—"

"They're not jumpers," he said, taking the reins of one horse from Shawn and holding them out to her, "but I think you'll find this horse a good mount."

She took a step back and felt her chest tighten. It hit her quickly, as it always did—that heart-pounding fear that overcame her and kept her from taking the step that could hopefully end the fear once and for all. "I...I... can't. I'm so sorry, but I can't." Out of the corner of her eye, she saw Shawn's shoulders droop, his disappointment clear. Even knowing that, she couldn't do what they expected.

Tanner handed the reins back to Shawn, and when the boy walked slowly to the barn with the horses, Tanner turned to her. "You just don't like cowboys or horses, do you? It's a shame, because Shawn was really excited about doing some riding with you."

He'd kept his voice low, but Jules didn't miss the disdain in it and had no choice but to defend herself. "That's not true. Cowboys have nothing to do with it. It's just that..." She stopped and took a breath, hoping to slow her galloping heart. "I love horses! But I can't ride, Tanner. I just can't."

When she started to turn, hoping they wouldn't hate her for running away, she felt him touch her shoulder. "Maybe you could explain?"

Unable to say more, she shook her head. But when she saw the look on his face, she knew he deserved at least some explanation. "I had a riding accident when I was a girl."

He looked at her as if waiting for more. "That's it?" He pulled off his hat and raked his fingers through his hair. "I can understand, but like you said, you don't hate horses or even cowboys. Maybe if you just—"

"No," she said. "I have to do this my own way, in my own time."

"You know, they say if you're thrown, you should get right back on."

To Jules, it was her former trainer talking, and she barely heard Tanner's words. Her trainer had pushed her too hard and too fast when she hadn't felt ready. She had never been able to stop blaming him for her accident, knowing her nervousness had played a big role in her horse's refusal at the jump.

Shaking her head, she took a step back, but Tanner continued, "We can help, Jules, if you'll just let us. We won't let anything—"

"Stop pushing me!" she heard herself shout. When she realized she had, it was too late.

# Chapter Five

The lunch crowd at the Chick-a-Lick Café was as big and noisy as usual. It had long been the gathering place for everyone in Desperation, from the time it opened for breakfast early in the morning, to well after suppertime.

Trying his best to ignore the chatter and clatter around him, Tanner looked up from helping his aunt into a chair to see Jules and Beth entering the café, and he wondered what he should say. The last time he had seen Jules had been at supper a week before, and the conversation had been strained. He had pushed her over the edge about riding, even though he'd only meant to help, and then he hadn't known what to say to her. Even after a week, he still didn't know how to tell her how sorry he was and how much he still wanted to help.

Bridey must have seen the two women at the same time, because she waved them over to the table. "You two come join us," she said. "There's plenty of room for two more."

When Jules looked his way, Tanner nodded, but a weak smile was all he could manage. Not that he wasn't pleased to see her, but he didn't know how she felt about what had happened.

"We can find another table, Bridey," Jules said, "but thank you."

"And just how long do you think you'll have to wait for that?" Bridey asked. "There's not an empty table in the place. No, you just sit with us. We're more than happy to have you both join us. Tanner can bring two more chairs."

Looking around the crowded café, Tanner wondered how he was supposed to do that. Every seat in the place was filled. With luck, he did find a spare chair at a table in the corner, and then one of the kitchen crew brought another from who knew where. Placing it on the opposite side of the table from Jules, Tanner settled onto it just as Darla, their waitress, arrived to take their order.

"Is the special still available?" Bridey asked.

"If you hurry," Darla answered. She looked harried. "Cook's trying to keep up, but for some reason, everybody in town decided this was the day to stop in for lunch. I've been running myself ragged since eleven, and it doesn't look to let up real soon."

After they'd each placed their order, they caught up with news and greeted friends and neighbors, until their food arrived. Tanner was pleased that he could then turn his attention to his meal, instead of trying to make conversation, most of which was centered around Beth's upcoming wedding.

"It was supposed to be a small ceremony," Beth was saying.

"Not in Desperation, Beth," Bridey said. "You know that as well as anyone else. Once you're a part of the town, everybody expects to be included in your most important events. Just wait until you have a baby!"

Beth laughed. "I think I'll hold off on that for a little while. I'm just glad Michael is from Geary. I doubt someone from a big city would understand."

Tanner glanced at Jules, who seemed to be agreeing. She also seemed to be having a good time. Bridey had noticed how quiet she'd been during supper the week before and mentioned it to him when Jules had gone home. She'd also given him what-for when he explained what had happened. Bridey didn't cotton well to poor manners, and she considered what he'd done to be none too good.

"I'm finding I enjoy small-town life," Jules said. "I spent a lot of time at Beth's family's small farm as a girl, but we rarely went into town. Desperation has so many nice people, and it's clear they all love Beth."

"Nothing not to love," Tanner said, finally able to offer a real smile. Now all he needed to do was apologize to Jules. But he still thought she was going about her fear of riding the wrong way. If she stayed around long enough, he was sure he could help her get over it.

"Why, thank you, Tanner," Beth said, blushing. "I've been meaning to ask when your next rodeo will be. Is it close by?"

"I leave the day after tomorrow for Pretty Prairie," he answered.

"Kansas?" Jules asked.

He nodded. "Maybe you ladies can make it?"

Beth shook her head. "I wish we could, Tanner, but there are so many last-minute things to do for the wedding that we need every second we have. If it wasn't for Jules, I don't know how I'd get everything done. I can't believe it's just over a week away! And you'd better be there, rodeo or no rodeo."

Wadding his paper napkin into a ball, he tossed it onto the table. "Oh, I'll be there. I wouldn't miss the professor getting hitched for anything."

Darla came by to refill the tea glasses and turned to Beth. "Your wedding is the talk of the town. If you need an extra pair of hands for anything, give me a call. I'm free of an evening."

"Thanks, Darla," Beth said. "We may do that as the day gets closer. So much to do, so little time." She added a sigh, but it came with a big smile.

When Darla walked away to check on other customers, Jules shook her head. "It's so amazing. In fact, it's…" She glanced at Shawn and grinned. "Well, *awesome* is the word that comes to mind. I can understand why you wouldn't want to leave here, Beth."

"Maybe you should move here," said Shawn, who'd been quiet throughout most of the meal.

"I almost wish I could," Jules answered. "But it would be a bit of a drive back and forth to Wichita every day. I'd be on the road more than in the office."

"We could always use another lawyer in Desperation," Shawn said, apparently not willing to give up the idea.

Tanner was amazed at how quickly the boy had taken to the woman. Tanner owed her a lot. Shawn had approached him the day after Jules had been there and had asked questions about his parents. Tanner didn't hesitate to tell him about the day Shawn's mother had left him at the ranch and to explain that he didn't know where his dad might be or what had happened to him.

Shawn had seemed a bit disappointed, but he said he

understood. "Maybe," he'd said, "someday we'll run into him at a rodeo."

Not wanting to get his hopes up, Tanner had told him that something like that was always possible and left it at that, hoping Shawn would accept that running off to find his dad wouldn't be the smartest thing he could do. Tucker could be anywhere. Or nowhere.

"We'd better be getting back," Tanner said, rising to his feet and reaching for his wallet. Tossing some money on the table for Darla's tip, he turned to Beth. "Give me your bills."

"No, Tanner, we'll take care of our lunch," Beth said, grabbing her bill from the table and reaching for the one left for Jules.

Tanner leaned across the table and snatched both from her hand. "Consider it a prewedding gift. It was nice to spend some time with both of you. Bridey gets tired of being stuck with us men."

Beth looked at Jules and shrugged. "No sense arguing. He's bigger than both of us."

Tanner laughed as he picked up his hat and placed it on his head, then headed to the counter to pay the bill. He finished the transaction at the same time the women stepped out the door, and he followed. "Do you have a minute?" he asked Jules.

She glanced at Beth and Bridey, who were deep in conversation near the car, parked diagonally at the curb. "Of course."

When he moved closer, she stayed put. This wasn't a conversation he wanted everybody in town hearing, and it would only take one person nearby to have it spread like wildfire. Taking a deep breath, he said what he knew he needed to say. "I want to apologize for not understanding about the riding."

She looked down before meeting his gaze. "No, please. It's all right."

He was relieved that she wasn't still upset. "Then I guess we're square on that. Next time I'll keep it in mind."

Her smile was soft and a bit sad. "I doubt there'll be a next time. I'll be leaving for home the day after the wedding."

He ignored the disappointment that hit him. "But you won't be a stranger," he said. "You know you're welcome at the Rocking O anytime. And next time I'll go easier on you."

"I'm sure you will, but it would be better if I do it my way," she said, glancing at Beth and Bridey. "I've put riding out of my mind for so many years it's going to take some time before I can get accustomed to just the idea of it. That isn't what I'd hoped, but…"

He looked to see what had grabbed her attention across the street, and when he realized what it was, he chuckled. "One of these days, she's going to catch him."

Jules turned to look at him, a bemused smile on her face. "What's going on?"

"That's Vern and Esther." He watched the two people crossing the street. The man in the lead kept checking back over his shoulder at the woman following him. When Vern picked up speed, so did Esther.

"They're married?"

"Not on your life," Tanner said with another chuckle. "But she's been after him for going on twenty years, I guess."

"Whatever for?"

"Your guess is as good as mine," he answered. "Nobody knows. Some say they had a thing in high school, and then he went away, joined the army and came back about twenty years ago. She started chasing him then, and he hasn't let her catch him yet."

"How strange."

"We have a few of those here," he admitted, "but no more than our fair share."

"I'd love to know what's behind it."

"So would everyone else in town, but most have formed their own ideas about what's going on."

"If you find out, let me know," Jules said, laughing. "It's absolutely—" Interrupted by the musical ring of a cell phone, she gave him a distracted smile and pulled the phone from her bag. "Well, hi," she answered, her eyes dancing with happiness. "I wondered when you'd get around to calling me."

Curious to know whose call pleased her so much, Tanner knew it wouldn't be polite to eavesdrop, so he backed up a step to let her know he wasn't. She immediately pulled the phone away from her mouth. "In case I don't get a chance to speak with you at Beth's wedding," she told him, "it was wonderful meeting you. I hope I'll get the chance to come back to Desperation again."

Speechless at the sudden brush-off, all he could do was nod as she went back to her phone conversation. Was this the end of it? Was Jules going to go back home and forget all about him, his family and the friends she'd made in Desperation? Watching her smile as she talked to the person on the other end of the line, he wasn't so sure she wouldn't. Instead of waiting around for her to finish, since she obviously didn't want him to, he joined his aunt and nephew, but not without a whole lot of questions going through his mind.

THE PERPLEXED EXPRESSION on Tanner's face before he turned away left Jules with a slight stab of guilt, but the phone call was important and something she couldn't put off. Placing the phone to her ear again, she forced thoughts of Tanner out of her mind before she spoke. "I'm sorry, Mom, what were you saying?"

"We're back in the States, and your father and I wanted to know how your vacation with Beth is going. And who were you talking to just now?"

Jules smiled, knowing full well that her mother's curiosity had gotten the better of her—the reason she had brushed off Tanner so quickly. "I'm having a wonderful time. With the wedding a little over a week away, Beth and I are swamped with last-minute details, and we're both wishing it would be here sooner."

Her mother's laugh was warm and loving. "Time will fly, as you'll soon see, and the wedding will be nothing more than a beautiful memory."

"It *will* be a beautiful wedding," Jules said.

"With you helping, who could doubt it? Now, who were you talking to?"

"A rancher friend of Beth's."

"Oh." The voice held disappointment. "Is he married?"

It was Jules's turn to laugh. "No, he's not. Not that it matters."

"Good-looking?"

How could she tell her mother just how good-looking Tanner was without her mother trying to encourage her to get to know him better? A *lot* better. "Very nice-looking, Mom. You'd say he's a hunk."

"Ooh, tell me more!"

Jules laughed again. "Maybe you should put Dad on the phone before he becomes as suspicious about you as you are about Beth's friend."

"He's paying the cab driver, but I wanted to touch base with you before we have to leave again."

Jules felt a small but familiar stab of disappointment. "I was almost hoping you might be here for Beth's wedding."

"I wish we could," her mother said, her voice sincere, "but we'll only be here for a few days, then we're off to South Africa to help with the AIDS Foundation there. I can't tell you how important that is, and I'm sure Beth will understand."

"Of course she will," Jules said, "but it still would have been nice to spend a little time with you."

"We will soon, sweetie, I promise. Oh, your dad said to tell you hi and that he loves and misses you. He's giving me the hurry-up sign," she said, chuckling. "I'll try to call you again before we leave, and I'm sorry I have to say goodbye now."

"I understand. Give Dad my love, and hugs to you, too." With a sigh, Jules closed her phone and returned it to her purse.

"Ready to go?" Beth asked.

Jules turned around with a smile and hurried to catch up with her friend. She was accustomed to her parents' comings and goings and the brief conversations, so she didn't let them bother her. She'd always known they loved her, and when they were together, they made every minute count. That would never change. Some people might find their lifestyle odd, but Jules had grown up with it and accepted that her parents felt the need to help others. She was thankful for that, even during the times she'd missed her parents the most.

"That was nice, running into the O'Briens," Beth said, as they walked on toward her house.

"Yes, it was," Jules said, thinking of Tanner's apology.

As if reading her mind, Beth said, "I noticed you talking to Tanner outside."

"And?" Jules asked, glancing at her friend.

Beth shrugged. "And I just wondered how that was working out."

"How *what* was working out?"

Beth's grin was wide and mischievous. "You know. You and Tanner."

"Aha! You *have* been trying to get us together. I knew it! Well, you can forget about it."

"Why?" Beth asked. "He's tall, dark and handsome, not to mention smart. What more could you ask for?"

Jules couldn't help but laugh. "You're right. He's all that and more, but there are several reasons why it wouldn't work. Do you want me to list them?"

Beth glanced around and then looked up at the sky. "It's a beautiful day and we have time. Please proceed, Counselor."

Still laughing, Jules gave it a moment of thought. "For one, there are other things in my life with much higher priorities right now. You know that."

"So if you didn't have those to think about, you'd be interested in, um, getting to know him better, so to speak?"

Refusing to answer because what Beth was proposing

wasn't a possibility, Jules continued, "For another, long-distance romances aren't all they're cracked up to be."

"It wouldn't be that hard to do, and you could always do what Shawn suggested and move here."

"Impossible."

"I don't see why," Beth countered.

But Jules saw no reason to discuss it. She'd thought long and hard about it after her outburst. She was firmly established in her career, in spite of the problems she was having, and there was no reason to pack up and start over in Desperation or anywhere else. "And for another," she continued, "we really don't have much in common."

Beth came to a stop in the middle of the sidewalk. "That's what makes it so interesting." Before Jules could say anything, Beth hurried on. "You can't honestly tell me you aren't attracted to him."

Jules gave an unladylike snort and walked on. "I'd have to be blind not to be, but attraction is a poor basis for a relationship, and I think that's what you're hoping for."

"I can't help it," Beth said, catching up with her. "You two were made for each other."

Shaking her head, Jules sighed. "I doubt that's the way he sees it, and neither do I. Give it up, Beth. He'll be gone until your wedding, and after that, I'll be gone. There's no time or even a reason to think anything will happen."

Beth shot her a catlike smile as they turned the corner to her house. "We'll see. I'd lay odds you'll soon find yourself missing him and will be back here in no time."

"I'll take that bet," Jules said, sure she would be the winner. Of course, she would miss him and all the O'Briens, just as she would miss Beth and everyone she'd met in Desperation. Once she was back home again, she hoped she would find that many things had been straightened out during her absence, but she wouldn't forget her visit to Desperation. In spite of what Beth thought or wanted, she really didn't see Tanner O'Brien in her life much longer, which was probably best.

"You'll lose that bet," Beth said. "Does twenty bucks sound good?"

Laughing as they reached Beth's yard, Jules nodded. "Very reasonable. But you'll be the one who'll be paying it."

"I wouldn't be so sure, if I were you."

But Jules was sure. As much as she was enjoying her stay in Desperation and the people, she hadn't conquered her fear, and there were too many other things going on in her life to even consider getting involved with someone. Someone she definitely found attractive and who made her heart race insanely whenever he was in the vicinity, but someone with whom she had nearly nothing in common.

BRIDEY GAVE TANNER *that look* as he slid into the church pew next to Shawn. He was late for Beth and Michael's wedding, but it couldn't be helped. Nothing had gone right all day, and he'd sent Rowdy ahead with Bridey and Shawn while he finished dressing. When he couldn't find his favorite tie, a tie he only wore for weddings and funerals, he almost gave up. Now that he was here, he almost wished he had.

At the front of the sanctuary, just to the left of the bride, Jules stood looking like a gift from heaven. But she wasn't a gift for him. He knew that. For the past week and a half, since he'd left her on the

sidewalk in front of the café, he had convinced himself that his attraction to her was nothing more than
a novelty. But seeing her again put the lie to that, and
now he didn't know what to do. Bronc riding had
taught him to focus, and right now the only thing he
could focus on was Jules.

He was both relieved and anxious when the ceremony ended and the wedding party moved back up the
aisle. At least he wouldn't have to sit there, battling to
keep his eyes and his mind off of Jules, but knowing he
would come face-to-face with her again in very little
time. There was still the reception to get through.

Thanks to the crowd around the newlyweds outside
on the church lawn, he managed to escape the traditional
receiving line without Bridey noticing. She'd give him
hell for it later, if she discovered it, but he didn't care.
He knew that sooner or later he would have to talk to
Jules, and their last conversation hadn't left him wanting
to kick up his heels with happiness. He'd spent the time
since then thinking, and then trying not to think when
he was on the back of a bronc. Her brush-off had been
what had made him so all-fired determined to believe
she was a passing fancy. Maybe she was, but seeing her
again left holes in that determination.

He was talking with several of the other ranchers in
the area about cattle prices when he glanced up to find
her looking at him. If it hadn't been for her smile,
cautious but hopeful, he would've stayed put and argued
the advantage of one brand of feed over another.

With a brief apology to the others, he stepped away and
approached her, his shirt collar and tie suddenly feeling
so tight he wasn't sure he could get a sound past them.

"It seems all I do lately is apologize," she said when he stopped in front of her.

Confused, all he could do was look at her. Finally he found his voice. "I don't understand."

"The phone call."

It took him a moment to realize what she was talking about, and then he wasn't sure how he should respond. "Okay," he said, with some hesitation.

"No, not okay." Her laugh was nervous and uneasy. "I'm sure it seemed very rude, and I didn't mean for it to."

He still couldn't think of anything to say that would make sense, so he just stood there, feeling like a fool. And the feeling didn't make him happy.

"You see," she went on, glancing left and right but not looking at him directly, "it was my mother, and I'm always careful about what she might overhear. Sometimes she's...well, let's just say that she can be very inquisitive and has a vivid imagination, especially when it comes to her daughter."

It took him a moment to understand what she was trying to say, but when he finally did, he was able to smile. "That's okay. No reason to apologize." And there wasn't, even though he wanted to know if Jules had mentioned him. He decided it might be pushing his luck to ask.

"My parents have been overseas for several months, so I don't get to talk to them often," she hurried on. "Sometimes they're between planes or on their way somewhere, so there isn't a lot of time for lengthy conversations..."

It all began to make sense. If it hadn't been for the relief he felt, her obvious nervousness might have given him pause. "I was kind of curious about the quick brush-off."

"Oh, no, it wasn't that," she assured him. "I knew we would see each other again. Here at the wedding, of course. I just didn't realize how I might have sounded until later."

"I'd have done the same thing," he admitted. And he would have. "Family is great, but sometimes they…"

"Make too much of things?"

"That would be it."

Her smile was sincere and lacked her earlier nervousness, causing him to relax, too. "How was the rodeo in Pretty Prairie?"

The change of subject to rodeo caught him off guard. He still wasn't convinced that she didn't like it, but he wouldn't make it an issue of it, since she was being nice enough to ask.

"It was good."

"Does that mean you won?"

"Well, I did bring home a nice-size purse for first place." He couldn't help but grin. As much as Rowdy liked to accuse him of wasting his time with smaller rodeos, instead of riding in a few of the bigger and more well-known ones, Tanner knew that in the long run, it was the points and purses that counted. And he was gaining every time he competed.

"That's wonderful."

He heard her sincerity, but he wasn't convinced of it. Not yet. But he might be able to find out. "Dodge City Roundup is next weekend. It's a bit farther away than Pretty Prairie, but you're welcome to join us."

Something changed in her eyes, but disappeared immediately. "Thank you, but I've been gone from the office for so long I'll be loaded down with work when

I return on Monday. I've already had calls about upcoming court dates, so I doubt I'll have time to do things I'd like to do."

So attending a rodeo and watching him compete was something she would like to do? Considering her reaction to the offer to ride that he and Shawn had given her, he couldn't believe she cared that much about sitting in an arena and watching him attempt to stay on the back of a bronc for eight seconds.

"There will always be others," he said, wondering if that really was true, at least for her. "If you have the time and want to go, that is."

"Of course I do. I keep thinking it might help, but so far, it hasn't," she admitted. "Maybe I'll manage some time later this summer."

He should have been pleased. At least she was willing, or at least said she was. But he couldn't find it in himself to feel positive about it. "Maybe you can."

When Michael and Beth joined them, Tanner was relieved. He spent a few minutes in conversation with them, and then was ready to call it a night. "I have an early morning tomorrow," he told them all, "so I'll say good night."

"So soon?" Beth asked, glancing at Jules.

"Afraid so. Congratulations to both of you," he told the newlyweds. "May the two of you enjoy many years together." He turned to Jules, not sure what to say, but he did his best. "It was a real pleasure meeting you, darlin'. If you do make it to one of the rodeos, don't hesitate to look me up."

Her smile instantly dimmed, and he knew she'd understood what he meant. He was convinced, finally, that this thing he had for her was going nowhere. He understood that, and he could live with it.

But later, at home, when the big ranch house was quiet and everyone else had turned in for the night, he sat in the ranch office, his thoughts still on Jules. Maybe he shouldn't have given up so quickly. He could have given in to those feelings he seemed to have for her—feelings that didn't seem to want to go away, no matter what he did or thought. He suspected there was something there for her, too. Maybe he should give it one more try.

If this thing between them lasted, he would be surprised, but other than having his hands full with Shawn, the ranch and bronc riding, there wasn't another reason he shouldn't give in and see where it took him. He doubted it would come to anything or last long. After all, most of his family—the people he cared the most about—had left him. In time, Jules would, too, but at least he knew that and wouldn't be so disappointed when it happened.

Was it worth the risk? Maybe. Did he want to try? He had to admit he did, even though he and Jules had very little in common. Maybe he should. But just how would he go about taking that risk now that she was back in Kansas?

## Chapter Six

Tanner spied the exit off the interstate into the city and deftly made the turn.

"Hey, we're not supposed to get off here," Shawn said. "This is Wichita. What's going on?"

Tanner glanced at him. "I've got a stop to make before we head on to Dodge City," he replied, his attention on the traffic.

"Where are we going?"

Tanner grinned. "Well, now, I figure it's going to get a little boring for you, sitting in the stands."

"It's never boring for me when you're competing."

Tanner could almost hear a pout in his voice. Shawn had been moody all week, ever since Jules had told them goodbye. He'd seemed like a different kid while she was at Beth's, but his often seen smile during that time had once again been replaced by a scowl. Nearly fifteen, Shawn still had a heap of growing up to do.

"So tell me—why'd you take that exit?" Shawn asked again.

Tanner chuckled, thinking of the plan he'd cooked

up. He'd either win or lose, but at least he wouldn't be left wondering. "A diversionary tactic."

"Huh?"

He glanced at his nephew. "You'll see." Watching street signs, he turned left. A few blocks later, in the midst of a commercial area, he took a right.

"Are you sure you know where you're going?"

"I hope so." At last he saw what he was looking for and pulled into the parking lot of an impressive office building. He got out and reached behind the seat, pulling out a shopping bag.

"What's that?"

Tanner smiled slightly. "A peace offering. Or a bribe. Depends on how you look at it."

Shawn regarded him with more interest. "For who?"

"Can't say." Tanner pulled his hat a little lower over his eyes. If his plan didn't work, he didn't want Shawn to be disappointed. "Just wish me luck."

Shawn slumped in the seat and stared at the dashboard. "Yeah."

With a sigh of frustration and a shake of his head, Tanner climbed out of the truck and started for the office building. The walk seemed like miles, and he could imagine how a condemned man felt on his way to the chair. The hot summer sun beat down on his back and shoulders, intensifying his feeling of dread. His palms were damp as he pulled open the heavy door and stepped into the cool, quiet lobby, looking around for a suite number. By asking Beth, who'd just returned from her honeymoon, he'd learned the office was located on the first floor, suite three. Time seemed to stand still as he searched the doors for a number. Mouth dry, he found the office and strode across the tile floor, the sound of his boot heels echoing off the walls.

*Dead man walking.* He shook his head to rid it of the notion. This wasn't a matter of life and death, but he was taking a risk. He hoped his pride was ready for a beating, just in case.

Taking a deep breath, he opened the office door and stepped inside.

Jules, her hands full of papers, was talking to a young woman seated behind a desk. She didn't seem to notice that he'd entered, and he took the moment to observe her. Polished and professional in a neatly tailored business suit, her hair in a twist at the back of her head, she was the epitome of a lady lawyer.

The woman at the desk looked up at him with a smile. "Hello. Can I help you with something?"

He shifted from one foot to the other, unable to think of what to say. "I...uh..."

Jules looked up, her eyes wide. Her mouth opened and her hand flew to her chest. "Tanner!"

He came to his senses and touched the brim of his hat. "Afternoon, darlin'."

Jules glanced down at the other woman—her secretary, no doubt—and back up again. "What are you doing here?"

Clearing his throat, he took a step forward. "Shawn and I are on our way to Dodge City, and I wanted to bring you a little something." He pulled the bag from under his arm and held it out.

Jules put the papers down and moved out from behind the desk. She stopped in front of him, her smile wobbly. "What is it?" She opened the bag and peered inside. Reaching in, she pulled out the black hat with the hammered silver band and turquoise stone. When she looked up at him, her eyes were misty. "Oh, Tanner."

"Here." He took it from her. To his surprise, his hands shook as he placed it on her head. The fit was a little snug.

"It's because my hair is pinned up." Her soft voice sounded thick with emotion. She smiled at him and turned around. "What do you think, Deb?"

The young woman ran an appraising eye over her and grinned. "Well, I can't say it goes with the outfit. On the other hand, you look terrific. It's a whole new you."

Jules turned back to him, her eyes shining. "Yes, it is. Thank you, Tanner. I don't know where I'm going to wear it, though."

This wasn't the place to talk. "Is that your office?" he asked, indicating an open door to her left.

She nodded, and he led her in that direction. Before going in, he turned to the secretary. "We'll only be a minute."

"I'm sorry, Tanner," Jules said when he'd closed the door behind them. "I don't know what's come over me." She took off the hat and held it in her hand, fingering the silver band. "This is just such a surprise. I didn't expect to see you again."

When she looked up, he couldn't read what was in her eyes. "Shawn and I are on our way to Dodge City. I'm entering the rodeo and I'll be riding tonight."

"I'll keep my fingers crossed for you." Her soft smile seemed almost wistful.

Her encouragement nudged him to continue. "No, darlin', that's not why I'm here." The look in her eyes was questioning. "I'm inviting you to come along with us for the rest of the weekend. We've reserved rooms at a local motel. Shawn can bunk with me."

A kaleidoscope of emotions crossed her face. "Oh, Tanner, I can't."

This could be the deciding moment. Either she was willing to see where this would lead, as he was, or she wasn't. Almost afraid of the outcome, he hesitated before asking, "Why not?"

"I haven't had enough time to get caught up from my vacation. I'm so far behind. Deb and I were just going over things I have to do when you walked in. I even had lunch in my office." She gestured to a fast-food sack in the trash. "I have appointments with clients all afternoon. I can't cancel them."

He felt a stab of disappointment, but it didn't dampen his determination. "How 'bout tomorrow?"

She shook her head. "I have to be in court first thing in the morning. I'm sorry. I really would like to go with you."

He stared at her, hope rising. "Yeah?"

She smiled in return, a little sadly, but a smile. "Yeah."

"Okay," he said, trying to think of an alternative. "What time do you finish up tomorrow? Can you come when you're done?"

"Late tomorrow, maybe," she said, her brow wrinkled in thought. "Yes, I think I can. I could drive out."

"No, darlin'. I'll come back and get you." There was too much danger of something happening to keep her from making the drive. "Give me directions to where you live. I'll pick you up sometime after seven."

"But what if you can't get away? If you're riding?"

Before he could answer, there was a soft rap on the door and her secretary stuck her head in. "Mr. Dayton is here."

Jules gave Tanner a pleading glance, before answering, "I'll be right with him, Deb."

When the woman was gone, he took her hat from her hand and placed it on her head again, giving the crown a tap. "Don't worry about a thing, darlin'. And get rid of those pins in your hair."

IT WAS AFTER SEVEN the next evening when Jules saw Tanner's familiar black pickup pull into the parking lot of her apartment complex. She watched him climb out, her heart giving a predictable lurch, and she reminded herself not to let this get out of control. She meant what she'd told Beth. They really weren't suited to each other. But she couldn't deny herself some time with him. If nothing else, it would prove she was right.

Not wanting to keep him waiting, she went to the bedroom for her suitcase. She was checking to make sure everything was turned off when she heard the knock on her door. She opened it to the most tantalizing smile she'd ever seen.

He stood, leaning against the doorjamb, one booted foot crossed over the other. "Evening, darlin'."

If she wasn't careful, she'd lose her heart just at the sight of him. "I'd say it's more like *'Night,* darlin','" she teased, opening the door wider.

Grinning, he shoved away from the door and ambled in. "Do you open your door to just anybody?"

"I knew it was you," she said over her shoulder as she grabbed a jacket. "I saw you pull up."

"I should hope so." He glanced around her apartment. "Shoot, Jules, this is more class than I've seen in a long time." His smile had changed to a slight frown when he turned to look at her. "You're used to the best, aren't you?"

"It's only me here, Tanner," she said softly, laying a hand on his arm. "I make a decent living, and I'm the only one I have to spend it on. Besides, I'm a great bargain shopper. You should see me in action." Bending to grab her bag, she felt him step up behind her.

He took the piece of designer luggage from her and she turned, their gazes locking. Her heart thumped until he finally spoke. "Shawn's waiting out in the truck."

She tore her gaze away and started for the door. "Good. I've missed him."

She saw him hesitate before a slow, lazy smile spread over his face. "He's missed you, too, darlin'."

He followed her out of the apartment and waited while she locked the door behind her. As they made their way down to the parking lot, she couldn't think of anything to say and was glad Shawn would be along to fill the silence. It would be almost three hours before they reached Dodge City.

Shawn beamed at her when they reached the truck. "Jules! Hey, this is great!" He climbed out of the truck and waited until she'd settled inside before getting back in again. "Boy, am I glad to see you!"

She soaked up the adoration. She'd have to remember this when she got to feeling down. Without a doubt, she'd never forget his welcoming smile.

Tanner chuckled softly and climbed into the truck on the other side. "Don't hold back, Shawn. Let Jules know you're glad to see her."

Shawn ducked his head, a sheepish grin visible under

his hat. "Sorry, Jules. I'm just happy you decided to come with us."

Jules laughed, thinking of the day before when Tanner had given her the hat. "You should have seen how surprised I was yesterday when Tanner walked into my office. If I could have come with you then, I would have." She turned to Tanner, acutely aware of him next to her. "It's a long drive. Are you sure you aren't too tired?"

Shawn answered for him. "No problem. We slept in late this morning. I guess he figured it might be a late night. And he doesn't need a lot of sleep. I've seen him—"

"Shawn?" Tanner said.

"Yeah?"

"You're gonna tire us all out real soon. Jules will be with us all weekend."

"Yeah, I know," Shawn continued as if he hadn't heard a word. "Did Uncle Tanner tell you he's in first place?"

"Tanner, that's wonderful!"

He shook his head. "We have a saying in our family, don't we, Shawn?"

The teenager slouched in the seat next to her, his chin sinking to his chest. "Uh-huh."

She looked from one to the other. "What is it?"

"'Don't spend your prize money before the last ride,'" Tanner answered when Shawn didn't.

Jules couldn't help but like the man. Sensible, kind, hardworking. What more could a woman ask for?

*A man who doesn't risk his life on a bucking horse every weekend.*

"Can I tell her about your ride?" Shawn asked before she could pay any attention to the nagging thought.

Tanner gave her a sidelong look. "That's up to her."

When Jules said she'd be delighted to hear about Tanner's ride, Shawn came to life again. Aided by Tanner, Shawn gave a blow-by-blow account of the high-scoring ride and how it had given him a bye for the night.

"He's wasting his time in Prairie Circuit," Shawn finished.

Jules felt Tanner stiffen beside her. "I'm sorry," she said, feeling like a fool, yet hoping to diffuse whatever was going on, "but what's Prairie Circuit?"

"It's just rodeos around here," Shawn explained. "Oklahoma, Kansas, Nebraska. All you have to do is take a look at his scores. He's good enough for major PRCA."

"That's enough, Shawn," Tanner said. "Circuit's good enough right now."

Shawn didn't answer, and Jules felt the sudden tension between the two of them. "You'll both have to educate me."

"It's complicated," Tanner answered.

"So explain it."

"Maybe later."

They rode in silence for a while, Jules wondering what it was about PRCA—whatever it was—and Prairie Circuit that could cause a problem between Tanner and Shawn. Tanner had asked for her help, but now he seemed unwilling to let her.

"I'm sorry," she said again, wondering if she'd made a mistake when she agreed to go to Dodge City with them.

"For what?" Tanner asked, glancing at her, before focusing again on the highway ahead.

Beside her, Shawn had fallen asleep and she felt safe to continue. "I didn't mean to cause any trouble."

"You didn't. The trouble was there before you."

"I might be able to help," she offered.

A soft smile eased the hard lines around his mouth. "You already have."

"At least tell me what the letters mean."

Tanner sighed. "PRCA is Professional Rodeo Cowboys Association."

"And what you're doing is different?"

"You're not going to let the subject drop, are you."

"Should I?"

For a moment he didn't speak. When he did, his hands gripped the steering wheel more tightly. "No, I guess you have every right to ask."

"If you don't—"

"No, it's all right. I owe you some kind of explanation. In years past, I competed in bigger rodeos. PRCA rodeos. Even earlier this year I started out that way. But as the months went by, I realized that Shawn needed my attention. And I needed to make sure he wasn't going to run off."

"He isn't going to do that."

"Maybe not now, but…" He shook his head. "Riding the smaller circuit keeps me closer to home. Shawn can tag along, like he is now. I'm doing okay, and there's a good chance I'll have enough winnings to qualify for National Finals in Las Vegas."

"You're doing everything you can to balance it all, aren't you?"

"I have to." Before she could say or ask more, he changed topics. "We're still a ways from Dodge. I don't mind if you go to sleep." She tried, unsuccessfully, to stifle a yawn. "Just lean up against me."

Jules sensed it wouldn't do to push for answers and gave in, resting her head against his strong shoulder. If only she could just stay here forever, she thought. If only she didn't feel gripped with fear at even the idea of climbing on a horse again. How could she have any future with this man if she couldn't conquer that fear?

WITH HIS HAND on the wooden door, Tanner leaned down to speak into Jules's ear. "They can be a pretty rowdy bunch after a day of rodeo. So stick close and ignore most of it."

"I've been in a bar before, Tanner," she answered with a chuckle. "We were introduced in one."

"Not like this one." He pulled open the door and let her walk ahead of him into the raucous room. Shawn followed and disappeared immediately. She stopped, and Tanner slipped an assuring arm around her. "Told ya."

The place was wall-to-wall people in a rainbow array of western wear. Hats of all colors topped the heads of every person in the room. Boots scuffed amid the sawdust on the floor to music that seemed to bounce over, under and through the crowd, while colored lights twinkled and twirled.

"What about Shawn?" Jules asked, looking around for him.

Tanner sighed. "Don't worry. The bar is in a separate area. No alcohol in this part of the place tonight. Come on." Keeping her close, he made his way through the mass of bodies to where he'd spotted Dusty, just as Shawn obviously had. Hailed by a large number of people, he acknowledged them with a smile or a wave, but didn't stop until they reached the table where the other two sat.

Dusty took a long look at Jules before shifting his attention to Tanner. "So this is the lady Shawn was telling me about." A wicked grin spread over his face. "Don't I know her from somewhere?"

Tanner pulled out a chair for her. "Ada," he answered without looking Dusty in the eye. "She was with Beth."

Dusty gave her a charming smile and winked at Tanner. "Uh-huh."

Tanner sat next to Jules and leaned closer, but he made sure they all heard him. "Remember what I said about ignoring most of it?"

Jules nodded.

He jerked a thumb at Dusty. "Start with him."

Dusty threw back his head and laughed. "That's classic down and dirty."

"You bet," Tanner returned with a grin. "Jules, meet one of the best bull riders in the country, who once claimed Desperation as his home, Dusty McPherson."

Dusty raised an eyebrow at Tanner before turning to offer her a smile.

"Jules Vandeveer," she said, offering her hand. "Are you competing in this rodeo, too?"

Tanner placed one arm along the back of her chair and reached out with the other to remove her hand from Dusty's. He'd held it a little longer than Tanner liked. "He's taking some time off to heal."

"Heal?"

Dusty leaned back in his chair and looked at Tanner, a twinkle in his eye. "I see you've staked a claim."

Tanner ignored the comment. "He's got a couple of broken ribs, so he needs to take it easy."

Dusty laughed again. "I get the message. But you won't mind if I ask her for a dance, will you?"

Leaning across the table, Tanner clearly stated, "She doesn't like country music."

"Tanner, I never said that," Jules protested.

Dusty scooted his chair back and stood, grinning. "That's because she hasn't learned to appreciate it yet. I'll give her a quick lesson."

Shawn jumped up from his seat. "Jules, let me teach you the Electric Slide. It's real simple." He smiled at Tanner and quickly led her to the crowded dance floor.

Tanner didn't take his eyes off her. And neither, he noticed, did several other cowboys in the room. Dusty had only been trying to rile him, but the others looked as if they might be a problem.

"I knew you had a thing for her back in Ada."

Dusty's comment brought him to full alert. Dusty might be his best friend, but he wasn't ready to tell him anything. "What can I say? She's different."

Dusty kept his eyes on the beer bottle he rolled between his palms. "It's nice to see you taking a real interest in a lady. Don't believe I've ever seen you so…"

"So what?"

Shrugging, Dusty shook his head and didn't say more.

Tanner's attention drifted back to watch Jules and Shawn trying the dance steps. Her long, blond hair swayed seductively across her back, and he realized she didn't know how beautiful she was.

"Is this going somewhere?" Dusty asked. "Is it serious?"

"Can't say. She's from a different world than you and me."

"But that's what gets your attention. She seems like a real nice lady. And Shawn sure has taken a liking to her."

Tanner turned back to watch them. The music had changed to a more upbeat rock tune and they'd joined the line dance. The steps had turned her to face in his direction, and he saw the pure joy on her face. It clashed with her lady-lawyer image. "Shawn's crazy about her."

"Reckon he's not the only one."

Tanner wasn't sure how to answer. He hadn't given any serious thought to a future with Jules. He wasn't sure he wanted to. "Commitments aren't my style," he reminded his friend. "You know my past record. First my mother, then Tucker. And let's not forget how fast Marlene took off when Shawn came to live with us."

"Marlene was a mistake you were lucky to be rid of."

Tanner couldn't have agreed more. To think he had almost married her made his stomach queasy. As soon as she'd learned Tanner had taken on the job of raising his brother's child, she couldn't get away fast enough. But Marlene was the past, and Jules was the present. Whether she would be the future was something he couldn't know.

"Jules is different," he said again, even though he hadn't planned on telling Dusty anything. "But who knows what will happen when the novelty wears off for both of us?"

"Maybe it won't."

Tanner met his gaze squarely. "Maybe you ought to find a lady of your own."

"Plenty of time," Dusty said with a wink and a shrug. "But it looks like you've found yours."

Tanner took a long drink of Dusty's beer and fixed his friend with a hard look. "She doesn't like rodeos."

"You can't ride broncs forever."

Tanner shook his head. "She had a riding accident when she was a kid and is scared to ride again. What kind of a future could an old cowboy think of having with someone like that?"

"People change. If it's important enough."

Tanner wasn't sure if he meant him or Jules.

The dance ended, and Shawn and Jules returned to the table. Tanner got to his feet and held out his hand. "I guess it's my turn," he said, and led her onto the dance floor. Pulling her into his arms, he looked down at the same time she looked up. Her smile alone could have melted the polar cap.

When he felt a tap on his shoulder a few minutes later, he was about to tell whoever it was to get lost. But it was Dusty.

"Shawn's pretty done in," his friend said in a quiet voice. "If he's gonna get some practice in with me tomorrow, he needs to get some sleep."

Tanner nodded and started to let go of Jules.

Dusty laid his hand on Tanner's shoulder and grinned. "I'll take him back to the motel and make sure he has enough sleep. You stay here and enjoy yourself."

"Thanks."

As Dusty walked away, Jules looked up at him. "Maybe we should go back to the motel, too."

"No need. We'll wait a bit until Shawn gets settled. A couple of hours of sleep will do me. I don't sleep much when I'm riding."

She frowned at him. "You probably should."

Without thinking what he was doing, he kissed the tip of her nose. "Okay, mother hen. But I've been doing this most of my life."

Concern filled her eyes. She started to speak, then shook her head, looking down.

He slowly ran his hand up and down her back. " What is it, darlin'?"

She hesitated. "I was going to ask something."

"So ask."

"It isn't important." She looked up with a smile. "Really it isn't."

"You look tired. Maybe we *should* call it a night."

"I am tired," she admitted. "This is the first time I've had a chance to relax since I returned to work. Then there's that small detail of your appointment with a horse tomorrow."

"A horse that doesn't like a cowboy on his back," he said, chuckling, as he led her off the dance floor and toward the door.

The weekend had only begun, and already he was feeling good about it and his decision to see where this would take him. Tomorrow would be the proof. Would she be a mental distraction for him, causing a poor ride, weakening what Rowdy referred to as his "edge"? Or would the opposite happen? He was willing to find out. Now. Before the relationship they were forming went any further. After that, there would be other things to deal with.

HURRYING AROUND behind the grandstand, Jules searched for Shawn. Only three more riders before Tanner's final ride of the rodeo, and the teenager had disappeared. It wasn't like Shawn to be gone at such an important time.

She'd expected him to join her earlier, but she hadn't seen him for quite some time. Not since Dusty had joined her in the stands for a while. She liked Dusty, but his presence had made her nervous, afraid he would sense her uneasiness around so many horses and riders.

Worried, she scanned the area, and then widened her search. She found a group of teenagers congregated in the parking lot and asked if they'd seen him. None of them had. Panic began to set in. She was responsible for him while Tanner was busy getting ready for his ride, and the boy was nowhere to be found. Tanner would never forgive her if anything happened to his nephew.

Cautiously entering the area behind the chutes near the stock pens, she heard someone call her name.

Dusty's worried frown was out of place on his usually grinning face. "What are you doing? You shouldn't be wandering around back here." He looked behind him as he took her elbow and led her around the pens. "Tanner expects you to be in the stands, not back here."

She looked up at him in the slowly fading daylight. "I can't find Shawn."

His fingers tightened on her arm, and he swore under his breath. "Tanner's ride is next. Come on, we'll watch the ride from here. Shawn knows to stay on the grounds. He's probably watching from the other side of the chutes. We'll catch up with him after Tanner's ride."

When Jules nodded, he steered her between a small group of cowboys to a fence that looked out into the arena. "If you sit on the fence, you can see really well."

"That's okay, I can see fine from—"

"Jules?" Dusty said.

She halted her retreat from the fence and looked at him.

"Does it scare you to watch him ride?" he asked.

Seeing the concern in his eyes, she hesitated. Reluctantly, she nodded.

He shook his head and sighed before pinning her with a serious look. "This is gonna sound cruel, but…"

She needed to hear what he had to say, even though she suspected she wouldn't like it. "Go ahead. Please."

Determination and apology joined the concern in his eyes. "Either learn to get used to it or get out of his life now."

His words hit her hard. She turned to gaze out at the arena, but didn't see anything through the threatening tears. He was right. Each time she watched Tanner ride, it was driven home to her a little more that she couldn't keep fooling herself. She either needed to accept who he was and what he did, or she should go back to her life before she met him.

Tanner was announced as the next rider, and she swallowed the tears blocking her throat, nodding to let Dusty know she'd heard him. He put his hand on her shoulder.

"If you need somebody to talk to, Jules, I'm here. Maybe I can help. My wife—" He broke off and offered a crooked smile. "My *ex*-wife felt the same way about my bull riding. I don't want to see anything like that happen to Tanner. Or you."

In front of them, the chute opened, and Tanner's ride began. Jules knew Tanner had given her the power to hurt him. She had seen it in his eyes. It was the last thing she wanted to do. But she didn't know how to avoid it. No matter what she did, she risked hurting him.

## Chapter Seven

Tanner growled into the depths of his equipment bag and ignored the other cowboys around him. He'd won the Dodge City bronc riding, but the joy over that hadn't compared with the joy of having Jules there. Since then, he'd spent the week on a high, and now he was coming back down. Jules was back in Wichita, and here he was in Ponca City, competing again. He was lonely. And that was strange, because he'd never felt that way before. In fact, it was usually the opposite. He never had a problem with being away from the ranch and enjoying his freedom, so he wasn't quite sure how to deal with this new sensation.

"Damn," he muttered into the bag, clawing through the contents.

"Lose somethin'?"

Frowning, he looked up to see Rowdy standing nearby, tossing the rosin bag in the air. Tanner straightened and took it from him.

"Found it in the pickup," Rowdy said.

Tanner mumbled his thanks, picked up his bag and turned to walk away.

"You know," Rowdy said from behind him, "you did real well last night. But if you don't stop thinking about that woman, you won't even make it out of the chute tonight."

Tanner stopped in his tracks and swore under his breath. He didn't need Rowdy needling him. And Rowdy knew it. Swinging around, he leveled his gaze on his foreman. "Her name is Jules. And she doesn't have anything to do with it."

"You can't tell me she doesn't have anything to do with this black mood you're in."

Rowdy's words stung, but Tanner wouldn't admit how close to the truth he'd come. "Everybody's entitled to a bad day," he answered, taking off again.

Rowdy grabbed his arm. "You can't have a bad day when you're planning to climb on the back of a bronc. You know that. When are you going to act like it?"

Tanner started to shake Rowdy off, but the fight went out of him. He did know better. He'd watched his own father slowly self-destruct because of a woman. A good ride didn't hinge on whether Jules was there to watch him or not. He'd be smart to keep his feelings about her—whatever they were—out of the arena.

Without turning to look at Rowdy, he nodded. "You're right."

He could feel Rowdy's satisfied smile.

"I'll meet you back at the motel later," Rowdy told him as he walked away.

The hot August sun beating down on him didn't lighten Tanner's mood as he climbed into his truck to head back to the motel. He hadn't slept well the night before, and memories of the ups and downs of his father's short career haunted him.

Brody O'Brien had wandered the circuit looking for his young wife, Sally, who'd run off and left him with two young boys. He never did find her. The hoof of a bull had connected with his skull and put an end to his quest and his life.

Brody had had the talent to be one of the best bull riders in the country, but because of Sally, he'd wasted it on small-time rodeos. His dream of someday making the National Finals faded with his obsession to find his wife.

Tanner wasn't a fool. He wouldn't do the same thing. Love, he'd learned at an early age, could destroy a man. Oh, he loved his nephew, his aunt Bridey and even his irresponsible brother, Tucker, even though he didn't know where he was or even *if* he was. But except for that love of family, he didn't believe in any other kind. Not for him. Love was something that destroyed. He had tried it once, and it had turned around to hurt him. Rowdy didn't need to worry. What he felt for Jules wasn't love. It was…well, it was…

It was just that she was good for him. That was all. And, damn it, he missed her.

Tanner threw his hat on the seat beside him and started the engine. He slammed the pickup into drive and hit the gas, spewing loose gravel from under his tires and making the rear end of the truck fishtail. He'd left Shawn back at the motel to take advantage of the amenities, and Rowdy was spending the afternoon with some old friends.

He slowed at the drive leading to the road, looked right, then left—and hit the brake pedal.

The car turning into the parking lot stopped next to him. Leaning his arm on the window edge, he waited for Jules to roll down her window.

Her eyes were hidden by a pair of dark glasses and her smile was tentative. "Hello, Tanner."

"Afternoon, darlin'. Out for a Saturday drive?"

Jules's lips turned up in a smile. "I, uh, thought I'd come down and watch the finals."

It wasn't that he wasn't pleased to see her, but the last time they'd talked, on the way back from Dodge City, she was certain she couldn't take the time off to come. Now she was here.

"For somebody who doesn't like rodeo all that much, I have to say this is a surprise." When her smile disappeared, he hurried to assure her. "Not that I'm not happy to see you. I was just headed back to the motel for a swim, a rest and Shawn. Follow me on over."

Jules smiled and nodded before easing her car forward and making a circle in the parking lot to stop behind him. With a quick glance in his mirror, he pulled out onto the road and headed toward the motel.

When they arrived, she pulled in beside his pickup, and he waited for her to get out of her car. When she didn't, he stuffed his hat on his head, climbed out of his truck and strolled over to meet her. Placing his hands on the roof, he leaned down to look at her through the open window. "I'm glad you came."

"I wasn't sure it was a good idea," she said. "Surprising someone like this doesn't always work out for the best."

He stared at his reflection in her sunglasses, unable to see her eyes. Reaching in, he slid the glasses down with one finger and caught her gaze with his. Uncertainty filled her green eyes. Popping open the door, he helped her from the car. "That's not something you have to worry about."

Her smile reached her eyes. "I need to get a room," she said as he closed the door. "I hope there *is* one."

"If there isn't, we can work something out." What came to mind wasn't something he thought would be best to share with her. And it wouldn't be a good example for his nephew. "I can always give up my room and bunk with Rowdy and Shawn."

"I wouldn't want you to have to do that. I can check in somewhere else if I need to. I don't want my being here or not being here to make a difference."

"It makes a difference. To me."

This time her smile was warm and loving. "I don't want it to make a difference in the way you *ride*. If you were forced to share a room with Rowdy and Shawn—"

"You worry too much. I won't let that happen."

She nodded. "We have enough differences between us."

He read the regret in her eyes and wondered exactly where it came from. "Being different has its pros and cons. You sure didn't hurt my ride last weekend in Dodge City, so all I know is that you're good for me. I haven't thought beyond that."

Closing her eyes, she nodded. "As they say, all good things must come to an end. Sometime."

Just hearing the possibility of losing her put into words caused him pain. Stepping closer to her, he placed his finger under her chin and tipped her head up, forcing her to look at him. "Maybe. Maybe not. I missed you, darlin'. It's only been...what, six days since Dodge City?"

"Five, but who's counting?" When he released her, she shaded her eyes with her hand, looking toward the swimming pool. "Is that Shawn I see?"

Tanner laughed and turned his attention to his nephew. "He keeps telling me we need a pool at the ranch, as if any work would get done if we had one."

"A lot of people with pools don't use them much," she said. "We never did."

The remark caused him to look back at her.

"I'd better go see about that room," she said quickly.

"Would you like me to go with you?"

She pressed her hand to his arm. "I'm a big girl, Tanner, I can get my own room. How long before you ride?"

"A while yet." Walking to his pickup, he reached for his bag and hoisted it over the side. "How long are you staying?"

"Through the weekend, if that's all right. I changed around some appointments to free up today," she said with a shrug. "Two had already canceled, which was what gave me the idea that I might be able to get away early."

"Maybe you should do that more often."

"Maybe I should. And maybe you should give that pool a try while I get a room."

"I think I will," he said. She left him with a smile that gave him hope. Not necessarily for anything permanent, but for now, he was ready to live for the moment.

He was enjoying a swim in the pool when she returned. "All done," she said when she reached the edge where he waited. "And there's no need for you to give up your room."

He hauled himself out of the pool and grabbed a towel from a nearby chair. "I'll help you with your bags."

"No need to do that. I pack light. I'm on the other side of the building, so I'll have to drive around."

Aware that they were alone, Shawn having gone to the room, he slipped an arm around her and pulled her closer. "Smart woman."

"You're all wet," she said, playfully shoving at his chest.

With a sigh of frustration, he let go of her. "Our timing couldn't be worse. I have to ride in—" Picking up his watch from a small table, he checked the time and frowned. "Too damned soon."

"Maybe I should go on to the rodeo grounds while you get ready."

"Yeah, maybe you should." He didn't want her to leave, but if she stayed a minute longer, he'd never make it back in time to ride, and he had a feeling it could be his best ride yet. He had his own satisfied smile when he thought of what Rowdy would think of it.

INSTEAD OF IMMEDIATELY finding a seat in the stands, Jules wandered around the rodeo grounds. Dusty had told her that the area behind the chutes wasn't a good place for her, so she was careful to steer clear of it. That didn't present a problem. She stayed far enough away from everything so she could watch the entrance to the parking lot to see when Tanner and Shawn arrived. Only then could she really watch the competition from the stands. She had managed the Dodge City rodeo all right, except for an ever-present queasy feeling in her stomach, but she had ignored it as much as possible. It was when she'd watched Tanner's rides that she had the most trouble. After her own accident and knowing how bad a fall could be, she couldn't stop worrying about him, even though she knew she shouldn't.

It wasn't long before she spied Tanner's black pickup turning into the parking area, pulling a horse trailer. Walking in that direction, she saw them stop and Shawn jump out of the truck.

"Shawn!" she called.

She knew he'd heard her when he turned in her direction, then pointed at her when Tanner and Rowdy got out of the truck. Tanner waved, and then turned to speak to Shawn, who then hurried her way.

"We're running late," Shawn told her when he caught up with her. "We might as well go find seats. Rowdy will stay with Uncle Tanner."

Seeing the wisdom in that, Jules nodded. "Lead the way."

It didn't take Shawn long to find them two good seats. They watched two other cowboys ride while Jules caught up with what Shawn had been doing all week.

"He's up next," Shawn said, nodding toward the arena.

"My fingers are crossed." She held up both hands as evidence.

She had a clear view of the chute. Because of the weekend before in Dodge City and what Dusty had said, she'd concentrated on becoming more accustomed to watching the sport Tanner loved so much, but she doubted she could ever enjoy it. It was something she knew she needed to work on, and maybe, once she overcame her fear of riding, it would be easier to deal with.

When Tanner's name and scores from his previous ride were announced, her nervousness kicked in.

Folding her hands in her lap, her fingers still crossed, she felt the familiar chill chase away the natural warmth of her body. *Here we go again,* she thought. But this was what he lived for, being bounced, jerked and pounded beyond reason, and she couldn't deny him the thing he loved. As she had the week before when she watched him ride, she took a deep breath, praying he stayed on for the full eight seconds.

When the chute opened, the noise of the crowd around her intensified, and she focused on the action in the arena. No matter what she might want to do, she would watch his ride until it was over and he was safely behind the arena wall again.

The bronc twisted and bucked beneath him, but Tanner stayed with the horse, his arm raised in the time-honored pose. Spinning first in one direction and then the other, the animal was determined to shake the weight from his back. Tanner held on.

"He's doing great!" Shawn shouted from beside Jules.

The ride was nearly over when the bronc took a sudden, unexpected twist.

"Damn," Shawn said beside her. "A suck back?"

"What?" Jules asked, shouting to be heard above the roar of the crowd.

"See how the horse twisted? That makes it really hard for Uncle Tanner to keep his seat."

Jules held her breath. Tanner slid to the side, and the bronc twisted again, throwing him in the other direction. But he still held on, attempting to right himself as the horn sounded the end of the eight-second ride.

Tanner let go of the rope and was tossed to the ground, and Jules let out the breath she'd been holding.

As he scrambled to his feet, the pick-up men took control and he walked away. The crowd thundered when his score of eighty-two was announced.

"Do you want to watch the next rider?" Shawn asked.

From the look on his face, Jules guessed he wanted to. She, however, only wanted to get to Tanner. While the leader readied himself for the last ride, she scanned the area behind the fence where Tanner had disappeared.

She couldn't spot him among those watching. "I think I'll go find him," she answered, "but you can stay if you like. We'll meet you at the pickup."

She pushed through the crowd and wove around the paraphernalia and people behind the stadium, knowing she was heading into forbidden territory, but not caring. She found Tanner, standing with his arms folded on top of the fence that looked out into the arena as the cowboy currently in first place finished his ride.

"Tanner?" she called to him.

He turned around to face her, a grin on his face. "There you are, darlin'. I was just getting ready to come find you."

"Shawn wanted to watch this last ride from the stands, but I wanted to see how you're doing."

As he walked toward her, the final rider's score was announced, and Tanner's grin widened. "Seeing that I'm now in first place, I'm doing pretty good." When he reached her, he put his arm around her shoulders. "But I have to admit that I'm worn-out after that ride. That was one tough bronc. I'm thinking about grabbing a bite to eat and skipping any celebrating."

"What? No honky-tonk tonight?" Jules teased.

"Not tonight, darlin'. I keep forgetting that I'm not

as young as I once was, but it's rides like that last one that keep reminding me."

"You're not that old," Jules said, looking up at him.

"I'm not that young, either."

"To be honest," she said, "I won't mind making it an early night, too."

From behind them came another voice. "I agree with that."

Jules turned to see Rowdy and Shawn, and she and Tanner slowed their steps to let them catch up. Rowdy seemed to be in good spirits, and there was no doubt that Shawn was eager to talk about Tanner's ride.

"What say we grab some fast food somewhere and take it back to the motel?" Rowdy said, stepping up on the other side of Tanner. "Rodeo's not over yet, and you have a full day ahead tomorrow. Won't hurt none of us to get some extra sleep."

They all agreed it was the best plan, and by the time they arrived at the motel with the food, it was getting late. They chose to eat their supper by the pool, and Jules enjoyed listening to the men talk about past rodeos.

When Shawn yawned for the third time, Rowdy nudged him. "Come on, boy, let's head to bed." He glanced quickly at Jules and then turned to Tanner. "You need to do the same real soon, too."

"I won't be long," Tanner told him.

No one spoke again until Rowdy and Shawn had disappeared into their room. "It's a beautiful night," Jules said, looking up at the sky, sprinkled with stars.

Tanner pulled off his boots and socks and rolled up his jeans. "Come on, let's go stick our feet in the pool."

"We really aren't supposed to be here so late." But she

couldn't resist and quickly removed her own boots and socks, ready to enjoy the water and the quiet of the night.

Settling next to each other on the side of the pool, they let their legs dangle in the water. Tanner leaned back, propping himself on his hands. "For a lady who doesn't like rodeo, you seem to be enjoying yourself."

Afraid to look at him, Jules stared at the play of nearby lights on the water. "It's definitely different," she said, and even tried to add a soft laugh.

"Maybe the time has come to give riding a horse again a try."

She'd known something like that was coming, and her whole body stiffened. "I can't do that yet, Tanner," she answered in a voice harsher than she'd intended.

"I only want to help."

His voice was gentler than before, and her breath hitched as she forced herself to relax. Maybe it was time to tell Tanner about her past so he could understand what she was dealing with.

"I was a competition jumper long ago," she began. "When I was twelve, my mount balked at a jump, and I sailed over his head." A shiver shook her, and she had to wrap her arms around herself to stop it.

He moved as if to touch her, but he didn't. "Were you hurt?"

Having recited it to herself and others a thousand times over the years, she knew how to answer without emotion. "I was in a coma for two weeks. When I came out of it, the injury had affected my speech. I couldn't talk."

"I'm sorry, I didn't know."

"Of course you didn't," she hurried to say. "There's no way you could know." She took a deep breath before continuing. "I'm the one who's sorry—for reacting so strongly."

"Like I said, I only want to help."

She knew he was being honest and sincere, and he deserved the same from her. Reaching out, she placed her hand on his. "You don't know how much that means to me. But there's more I should tell you."

"What's that, darlin'?" he asked, turning his hand to lace his fingers with hers.

"It's… I think you should know that I'm concerned you might get hurt." Before he could say anything, she hurried on. "I know it's partly because of my fear of riding, but it's also because I know just what can go wrong in a split second."

"Accidents happen," he said, brushing his lips across the back of her hand. "I'm an experienced rider and I know the risks I'm taking. Anything worth doing has a risk."

She knew he was right, but she still wasn't ready to take that risk and move on with her life. She wondered if she ever would be and if that would affect the way they felt about each other. It was all the more reason she needed to screw up her courage. But that was something more easily said than done.

THE NEXT AFTERNOON, Jules sat on the pickup tailgate between Dusty and Tanner in the parking area of the arena, watching Shawn rope a makeshift dummy calf. She'd taken an instant liking to Dusty and was glad he'd joined them that morning. Even after he'd taken her to task, she considered him a friend. She'd needed that push to decide whether to put an end to what she'd begun to think of as a relationship with Tanner or to see where it would take her. She was glad now that she'd decided on the latter.

"He's a natural," Dusty said. "Won't be long before he'll be begging to enter," he went on when no one commented. "I can't put him off much longer."

"He's not even fifteen yet," Tanner said. "There's plenty of time."

Dusty shifted on the metal. "You're not going to solve anything by holding him back. Lots of kids are already competing."

"He's still too young."

Jules glanced at Tanner and saw the stubborn set to his jaw. After spending time with Shawn, she knew the teenager resented his uncle's resistance to his getting involved in much rodeo.

"Tanner," Dusty said, his voice low, "Shawn's not going to run off like Tucker did just because you let him—"

"I guess it's my decision." Tanner stood and walked away from them, his back straight and proud. "Pay attention to what your horse is doing," he shouted to Shawn.

Dusty grunted beside Jules. "He's as stubborn as that old mule Rowdy."

At the mention of the foreman's name, Jules sighed. "I don't think Rowdy likes me very me much."

"Rowdy doesn't always know what's best for Tanner."

She turned to see Dusty studying her, his eyes serious. "If you're referring to me, that remains to be seen."

"Not if those broncs haven't bucked all the sense out of him." He turned to look at Tanner and Shawn. "'Course sometimes I do wonder if they haven't already."

Not sure what Dusty meant, Jules remained silent and watched the action in front of them. Tanner stood with his legs spread and firmly planted while he shouted instructions at his nephew, whose scowl had reappeared, replacing his excitement of the night before.

Suddenly Shawn dismounted, threw his rope on the ground and stomped away. "Forget it!" he shouted over his shoulder.

"Shawnee!" Tanner bellowed. The boy stopped but didn't move to look his way. Tanner's voice dropped. "Why don't you let Jules get acquainted with Sundancer?"

Shawn answered with a curt nod and tied his horse to a post.

Jules turned to Dusty. "Who's Sundancer?"

Mischief danced in his eyes. "The extra horse they brought."

She jumped off the tailgate, her hand in front of her to halt Shawn, who was approaching her and leading a horse. "Oh, no," she said. "I am not getting on a horse."

"You don't have to get on her if you don't want to," Shawn said. "Just come get used to her. Uncle Tanner won't make you ride and neither will we."

Tanner had disappeared. Just as well, she thought. He'd only have reason to be disappointed in her, and there were already enough obstacles between them without forcing the horse issue again.

Still, he'd know soon enough. Taking a deep breath, she turned to Shawn. "Oh, all right."

Shawn held the reins out to her. "Why don't you lead her around? Let her get used to you. You don't have to get on her."

"That's okay." Jules shook her head and took a step

back. The temptation was strong—she yearned for the years she'd ridden—but not strong enough.

Before she knew what was happening, an arm caught her around the waist and scooped her off her feet and into the air. She let out a shriek and found herself atop a horse, Tanner behind her, his strong arms wrapped securely around her.

His warm breath caressed her ear. "I won't let anything happen to you, darlin'. You know that."

Fear left her without a voice, and she could only nod. Trembling from head to toe, she closed her eyes and prayed nothing would happen.

"Swing your leg over," he whispered.

"I can't," she whispered back, her eyes squeezed shut.

"Jules," he said patiently, "I've got you. I'm holding you tight. You are not going to fall. I'd have to fall, too, and that isn't going to happen. And this horse isn't going to throw either of us. I promise."

She had to admit he had a point. After all, the man rode bucking broncs and managed to stay on. It would take more than her to topple him off a horse.

"Okay," she squeaked. Saying another quick prayer, she opened her eyes just enough to see and slowly moved her leg over the horse's neck. Still shaking, but feeling a triumphant satisfaction, she sighed.

"Hang on to the saddle horn and just lean back and relax against me."

She obeyed, except for the relaxing part. That was asking just a little too much. Beneath her, the strength of the horse was evident. But so was Tanner's broad chest behind her. She let go of a bit of her fear. They moved forward, and she slammed her eyes shut.

Memories of her fall filled her mind, and she opened her eyes to ward them off.

"Tanner?" Her voice squeaked again.

"We're just going to walk around a little." He pulled her hat from her head and tossed it to Shawn, who stood grinning at them. "Give Sundancer a little workout," he told his nephew. "We'll be back later." Moving the reins, he turned them around. "You okay?" he asked her.

"I think so." A feeling of safety and contentment began to suffuse her. "You might have warned me, though."

"Wouldn't have worked if I had."

Knowing he was right, she didn't argue.

They rode slowly around the parking area, saying little, and Jules found herself feeling more at home again on a horse.

"Ready to try it on your own?" he asked.

That was a little more than Jules was ready to attempt. "Not quite yet. But it isn't nearly as bad as I thought it would be. I guess it really is true that the apprehension is usually much worse than the actual event."

He nudged the horse into a trot. "Tell me if it bothers you."

Surprised that it didn't, she laughed softly. "It's wonderful." Turning her head to look back at him, she sighed. She'd been foolish not to completely trust this man.

He pressed his lips to her ear and whispered, "Glad to help, darlin'."

By the time they joined Shawn and Dusty again, she had begun to feel the joy that riding had given her as a girl. She might not be ready to try it on her own, but she had taken the first step, thanks to Tanner.

Still, the matter of her riding wasn't the only obstacle between them. Her fear of his bronc riding was an issue that wasn't going away.

# Chapter Eight

"Shawn is going to Coffeyville with us."

Tanner's clear voice drifted out the screen door to Jules, who waited patiently with Bridey on the wide porch of the ranch house. Trying not to listen, it was impossible not to overhear, and she couldn't help but hear Rowdy's response.

"You're *rewarding* the boy for getting in trouble?"

"Do *you* want to stay here and babysit?" Tanner countered.

Rowdy's mumbled reply couldn't be heard, but Tanner's response could, his voice rising with his clipped, staccato statements. "No, she's here to go to the rodeo. With us. With *me*. Not to take care of Shawn. He is *not* her problem. He's mine. And I say he goes with us. Now, I've got some broncs to ride."

"Then let's talk about *that*."

"About what?"

"You know damn well what. You want to tell me what happened last weekend?" Rowdy asked.

There was a moment of silence, and then Tanner said, "I don't know."

"We need to figure out what went wrong."

"Not now."

"Look, boy—"

"I said, not now! And I'm not your 'boy.' "

Standing next to Jules, Bridey let out a heavy sigh. "I swear," she muttered.

The conversation inside continued to drift outside. Even knowing she should walk away, Jules couldn't make herself do it. What would Bridey think if she did? What was she thinking when she didn't?

"No, you're not my boy," Rowdy was saying, his voice calm and a little sad, "but you're the closest thing to it I've ever had. And we're going to use that ride to learn something."

"Later."

There was the sound of heavy footsteps, and then it stopped. "You know what it was that caused it. Admit it."

"I don't know anything except that I have a rodeo to get to."

"It was because of her," Rowdy said. "You lost your concentration. And that danged bronc knew it and took advantage of it. Admit it."

"That isn't what happened, but if that's what you want to think, go right ahead. And if you remember, I took first place."

Heavy footsteps advanced in the ensuing silence, and Rowdy slammed out the door, muttering to himself. Jules had to jump back to keep from being hit by the flying screen door. She'd known things weren't going well. Tanner had told her about Shawn breaking curfew the night before, out with friends Tanner didn't approve of.

"It's not unusual that he did it, Tanner," she had told

him. "Don't worry about it too much. It's typical end-of-summer limit testing. Once he's back in school…" She'd hated to say it, but he needed to hear it. "Maybe getting him more involved in rodeo would help."

"Maybe," Tanner had replied. "And maybe not. Right now it's a wait-and-see thing. He knows that, but he's pushing it."

Shawn, however, wasn't what Jules was worried about at the moment. Rowdy's words had hurt her deeply. For whatever reason, the older man didn't like her and probably never would.

Wishing she hadn't overheard the argument, she knew she needed to do something. Since the moment she'd arrived at the ranch the evening before, she'd been only too aware of Rowdy's growing disapproval. And she noticed how it affected Tanner. She feared the tension between the two men would not only affect Tanner and his relationship with Rowdy, but his riding, too.

Taking a deep breath, she reached for the door handle, but as she did, Bridey laid a hand on her arm, stopping her.

"They're both muleheaded, Jules, but they'll work it out in time," she said quietly. "Shawn is Tanner's responsibility, and he and Rowdy don't see eye to eye on raising a young 'un. Never have. Rowdy will give in sooner or later, after he's had his say, and Tanner will do what's best, no matter what Rowdy says."

Jules knew Bridey was trying to downplay what Rowdy had said, but they couldn't ignore Rowdy's feelings about her any longer. "Thank you, Bridey, but we both know this doesn't really concern Shawn. It's *me* Rowdy doesn't like."

"It isn't you, either. And it isn't any of his business." With a loud sniff, she turned to step off the porch, heading in the direction Rowdy had gone.

Jules gathered her courage and pulled the door open. She needed to discuss this with Tanner. Not that she wanted to, but it had to be done. She couldn't just stand around like a little mouse while trouble was brewing because of her.

Stepping into the dim entryway, she saw Tanner walking toward her. The sun from the adjacent living room accented his frown and the worried crease of his forehead. His hat in his hands, he strode straight at her, but she knew he hadn't seen her.

"Tanner?"

His gaze sought her out in the shadows. He smiled, but it didn't reach his eyes. "Ready to leave, darlin'?"

Jules pulled her own hat from her head and fingered the brim. "Why don't I stay here this time? Or go home. You go with your family this weekend, and I'll wait until next."

He looked at her with stony eyes, his jaw hard, his lips a thin line. "Are you backing out on me?"

She wouldn't hide from the truth any longer. "No, but I don't want to be the reason for any trouble. I…" She stopped and took a calming breath. "I heard what Rowdy said. You don't need the stress my presence is causing."

Putting his hat on, he reached out and slipped his free hand to the back of her head before sliding his other arm around her waist and pulling her close. "There'll be a helluva lot more stress for me to deal with if you don't go."

"But Rowdy—"

"Rowdy be hanged," he growled. "The old buzzard

doesn't know his head from his backside sometimes. I asked you to come with us. I don't give a hoot what he thinks. What *I* want and need is what counts."

Arguing wouldn't change his mind. Bridey was right. Both men were stubborn. "All right," she whispered. "If you say so."

"He'll come around." His kiss was light, but offered hope.

"Why don't I take my car?" she suggested as he walked her out onto the porch, his arm now around her shoulders. "Bridey can ride with me, and you men can take the pickup. We can have some girl talk without boring you."

"You're letting him win, Jules."

"It's not a war, Tanner."

With a force to match his mood, he closed the heavy wooden door behind them and locked it.

Jules could only hope he was right about Rowdy coming around, but she wasn't counting on it.

"YOU'RE LIMPING."

After Tanner's ride that evening, Jules and Bridey had exchanged fried-chicken recipes while they'd waited for the men. When the three approached, Jules noticed Tanner favoring his right leg.

"Are you all right?" she asked him after he planted a quick kiss on her cheek.

"It's nothing, darlin'. Just my old knees." Taking her by the hand, he circled her car, and she noticed him wince when he helped her inside it.

"You *are* hurt," she said as he closed her door. "Maybe you should see a doctor."

"It's just my knee," he snapped. The flash of impatience in his eyes was replaced by contrition. "It got whacked a little too hard in the chute. I'll put some ice on it when we get to the motel, and it'll be fine by morning."

Shawn helped his aunt into the car on the other side. "It really isn't a big deal, Jules. Happens all the time. But I guess we won't be going out tonight." His disappointment was clear.

When Shawn joined the others, Tanner reached back to tug at the brim of the teenager's hat. "Jules can keep me company while the rest of you go out and have a good time."

The sound of Rowdy clearing his throat behind Shawn stilled all of them. "We can bring you both back something to eat before we go out and keep you off that knee."

"Thank you, Rowdy," Jules told him with a smile. His answering nod was brief, but she felt a sliver of relief. At least he hadn't demanded that he be the one to stay with Tanner.

The drive was short, and when they arrived at the motel, they split up into separate rooms. Shawn was allowed to take Jules's car to get a cooler and bag of ice, with Bridey along as the adult driver, while the others changed into fresh clothes. Jules switched her jeans and top for a T-shirt and pair of shorts, and then waited on Tanner.

When he emerged from his room, he'd changed into a pair of jogging shorts and T-shirt with the sleeves cut off, looking even more different than he had the weekend before in the pool.

"This can't be Tanner O'Brien, champion bronc rider," she teased.

He slung an arm over her shoulders and steered her

to the outdoor pool, laughing. "The costume may have changed, but the man is the same."

They settled in side-by-side chaise lounges at poolside. At the far end of the pool, three small children could be heard voicing their objections to their mother's insistence that it was time to call it a night. Tanner's chuckle at their protests made Jules smile.

"I'll bet you were good with Shawn when he was small," she said, watching his enjoyment of the scene.

His smile wavered, but his gaze remained on the children. "Wish I could say the same now."

She reached over to squeeze his hand. "You do fine. "He's at a tough age, that's all."

They both watched in silence as Shawn drove into the motel lot and parked the car, and then pulled out a cooler that he took into the room he shared with Rowdy. Bridey said something to him at the door, turned to wave at Jules and Tanner, and walked on to the women's room. In a few minutes, Shawn reappeared, loaded down with an ice bag and towel in one hand, and a glass of water in the other. His walk had a certain swagger.

"Rowdy said to be sure to keep this full of ice." He placed the bag and towel next to Jules and handed Tanner the water and some pills. "And take the aspirin every three hours."

"I'll make certain he does," Jules said.

Shawn turned to grin at her. "We'll stop by with some food later if you don't mind waiting."

"Not if you bring out some beer," Tanner told him.

Jules leaned around Shawn to look at him. "Beer and aspirin?"

Tanner grinned at her. "Shawn, bring the beer."

When Shawn disappeared, Tanner spoke without looking at her. "I know women have a built-in mothering thing, but I don't need a mother, darlin'."

Properly chastised, but needing to show him she had no intention of playing mother, she picked up the towel and ice bag. "Tanner?" He turned to her and she tossed both at him. The ice bag landed square in his lap.

He yelped and grabbed the bag. While she laughed, he glowered at her, and then placed the bag on his knee, wrapping the towel around it.

Shawn reappeared with two cans. "Here's your beer, Uncle Tanner, and a soda for you, Jules." He passed out the drinks and waited.

From behind them, Rowdy called out, "Come on, Shawn, let's get going before they run out of food."

Shawn waved at him before focusing on Tanner. "If you need anything…"

"Jules will take care of me," he answered with a quick wink at her. "You all have a good time."

Shawn nodded before telling them both goodbye and joining Rowdy and Bridey. Jules and Tanner watched them drive away.

"He *is* a good kid," Tanner said as the taillights disappeared.

"That's obvious."

After a short silence he went on, "It's been a bad summer for him."

"You've done a good job, Tanner. Don't ever think you haven't."

"He's got the same wild streak Tucker had, and it's why I'm not ready to let him enter any rodeos yet. That's how we lost Tucker. Do you understand?"

"I think so." What she understood was that Tanner blamed himself for Tucker's disappearance. "But it isn't because you did something wrong."

"If I hadn't been so busy with my own interests, it wouldn't have happened." His harsh voice conveyed his disappointment in himself. "I wanted to do nothing but rodeo and spend time with Marlene."

Her throat closed. Of course there had been women before she'd met him, but hearing a name made it more real. "Marlene?"

"Forget it."

If only she could. But he didn't seem inclined to discuss it, and she wouldn't ask. There was enough of his past to deal with, not to mention her own, without adding to it.

She stood and held out her hand. "Let me get some fresh ice."

He unwrapped the towel and handed her the ice bag. She felt his gaze on her and reluctantly met it. His expression was unreadable, but she felt it deep within her, making her heartbeat quicken. "Shall I bring you another beer?"

He shook his head, and she hurried to the room. Maybe she'd been crazy to agree to stay with him. It wasn't the type of relationship she was looking for. But then, she hadn't been looking for anything. Still, if she had been, it wouldn't have been a bronc-riding cowboy she'd probably never understand. Love did funny things to people.

Her hand froze on the ice on its way from cooler to bag. *Love?* Good heavens, she didn't love Tanner! But as she dropped the ice in the lip of the ice bag with trembling hands, she knew she was lying to herself. No matter how different they were, she *had* fallen in love with him. Despite her fears for him with his chosen career, she'd agreed to join him and follow and cheer him on. Only a woman in love would do that, and she'd done it with all her heart.

Somewhat dazed at her self-revelation, she returned poolside to find that her seat had been flipped in the opposite direction, still side by side with Tanner's, but now she'd be facing him. She handed him the ice bag in silence and sat down while he reapplied his wrap. Leaning forward to do it, his shoulder bumped hers and she felt the warmth she always felt at his slightest touch.

When he finished with his knee, he focused his attention on her. Raising his hand, he stroked her cheek. "I wanted to be able to look at you," he said, leaning back, his palm cupping her face. "Too bad we couldn't go out and have some fun with the others, but I need to take it easy with the knee until after tomorrow."

"See? I knew you were hurt more than you would admit."

Grinning, he chucked her under the chin before taking her hand. "Nothing I can't handle and haven't before."

His thumb caressed the back of her hand, and she closed her eyes, listening to the quiet sounds of the evening.

"I suppose it's time I told you about my family," he said, his voice low and unsteady.

Surprised, she opened her eyes and looked at him. "I thought you had."

"Not all of it. Not about my parents."

Jules wasn't sure what to say. "Only if you want to tell me."

"My mother is full Cherokee."

"That explains a lot."

His sparkling blue eyes were set off by the tanned crinkles around them when he grinned at her. "That and the O'Brien Irish." His grin disappeared, along with the laugh lines, as he continued, "My grandmother Ayita still lives on the reservation in Tahlequah."

"Do you visit her often?"

He shook his head. "No."

"But—"

"She and my grandfather, Adahy—he's called Sam—had one daughter. Salilah, or Sally, as everybody called her, was seventeen and an up-and-coming barrel racer. Then along came Brody O'Brien, Bridey's twin brother and my father. He'd already made a name for himself as a bull rider."

"Rodeo has obviously played a big part in your family history," Jules managed.

"You could say that," he said with a rueful smile. "People say Sally was a beautiful child."

"I'm sure she was."

"Yeah, but she was a kid. If Sam and Ayita had just told them no..." He shook his head from side to side. "Funny how things happen. Sally was only seventeen when Brody, who was eight years older, asked her to marry him. Sam and Ayita didn't want her to marry so young and asked them to wait until she turned eighteen. Brody adored her, so he honored their wishes. He took the money he'd been saving from his rodeo winnings and bought the land that's now the Rocking O. It wasn't long before he quit rodeo to settle down and ranch, and Sally continued to compete, but a year after they got married, she had me. When she turned nineteen, she ran off. All she wanted to do was rodeo. She was just too young to be a mother."

"Oh, Tanner," Jules cried, "I'm—"

"Nearly broke Ayita and Sam's heart. My daddy's, too, so he hired a private detective who found her traveling with a rodeo and brought her home. To make a long story short, Sally got pregnant with Tucker, Shawn's daddy, and after Sam died a few years later, she took off again, leaving Tucker and me with our dad. That's when Bridey came to live with us. She'd lost her husband to cancer and needed her family, and my dad couldn't raise us alone. It wasn't long before he left to hunt for Sally."

Jules noticed how Tanner called his father his dad, but referred to his mother by her name. "Did he find her?" she asked in a hushed voice. "Have you seen her since?"

At some point, Tanner had let go of her hand and sat upright in the lounger. He shook his head. "My dad was killed bull riding when I was fourteen. I don't know what happened to Sally. From what I was told, she never returned to the reservation. She hated it there. I think she married my dad to get away from it, but I don't know. Don't really care much, either."

"It must have been hard for everyone," Jules said, imagining how the family must have learned to cope.

Tanner continued as if she hadn't spoken, "I already told you that Tucker ran off when he was fifteen. Shawn will be fifteen in three months, so maybe you can understand why I worry about him and some of the decisions he makes."

Jules nodded. "Of course I do. You don't know where either one of them are? Tucker or Sally?"

"They both just disappeared," he said, his voice

without emotion. "When I was a kid, I always thought she might have joined up with a tribe somewhere when she got older, but that was a little boy's imagination. As for Tucker...I did all I could to try to find him. Spent a fortune on private detectives."

"I'm sure you've done everything you could."

He didn't seem to hear her, as if he was lost in the past and the memories. "I guess I'm just destined to be alone."

Reaching out, she placed her hand on his arm. "You aren't alone, Tanner." When he turned to look at her, she saw the desolation in his eyes and knew he needed her to say the right thing. "You may not have a traditional family, but Bridey and Shawn *are* your family."

Nodding, he took her hand in his and held it. "Has anybody told you what a good person you are?"

Her answer was a smile. Until she thought of Joey and how his mother had reacted and blamed Jules. Now Jules wasn't sure if she had what it took to make the best decisions, either.

But this was about Tanner, not her, and she needed him to know that he wasn't alone. "Look how much you're respected by your neighbors and friends," she pointed out. "That counts for a lot, you know."

For a moment he didn't respond, but when his gaze met hers, she knew he understood what she was saying.

"I'm a pretty lucky man, I guess." Leaning back, he pulled her out of her lounger and sat her next to him on his. "Before school let out, I was traveling more and doing pretty good. Riding high, you could say. But I saw I needed to keep an eye on Shawn. Rowdy may not agree, but it didn't hurt me a bit to stick closer to home, rather than traipse all over the country.

I'm not far from qualifying for National Finals Rodeo in December."

"So if it hadn't been for Shawn—and Beth—we might never have met?"

"That's about it, darlin'."

She laughed at the memory. "Remind me to thank him."

"I'll do that," he said with a sexy chuckle.

It had only been a few weeks since she had first seen Tanner and Shawn together in the parking lot in Ada. "Shawn's making good strides, Tanner. I know you don't see it, but he is."

"Yeah, I guess he is. I'm just impatient and want so much for him." He pulled her down to his chest, his lips only a breath away from hers. "And so much for me, too."

Before she gave herself up to his kiss, she wondered just what he wanted for himself. Could it be possible that she might be a part of that? And if so, was she ready?

When his ride was over on Saturday night and he'd won the bareback-bronc competition at the Coffeyville rodeo, Tanner's first thought was to find Jules. He accepted that Rowdy had a point that she might be a distraction, but as far as he was concerned, she was his good-luck charm. And no matter what Rowdy might think, when he climbed into the chute, his mind was on the horse beneath him and making it to the buzzer at the end of the eight seconds.

He found her behind the announcer's booth, waiting and watching for him. Her smile when she saw him made his heart jump with happiness. How could he be so lucky?

"Are we going to party?" she asked as he slipped an arm around her.

"Is that what you want to do?"

She looked up into his eyes, and he tried to read what was in hers. "Whatever you all decide," she answered.

Turning her in his arms to face him, he shook his head. "No. Tonight it's all about what *you* want to do."

She hesitated for only a moment. "I'd like to spend time with you. Alone."

His heartbeat quickened, but he forced himself not to hope. He'd only be ready when Jules was. "Any-place special?"

He felt her take a deep breath, and then she locked her gaze with his. "Your room or mine. It doesn't matter."

The desire in her eyes was clear, but he didn't want to rush her into something this important. "You're sure?"

Nodding, she smiled. "Very sure."

For a moment he couldn't breathe. He'd tried not to think about this happening, but the more time they spent together, the more he wanted her. He just hadn't wanted her to think that was all she was to him.

Leaning down, he kissed her, but kept it brief. There would be time for a real kiss later when they were alone. "Can we take your car?"

She pulled away and dug into her purse, pulling out a key ring. "As long as you drive."

"I think I can manage that," he said, taking it from her.

They headed toward the parking area, and when they arrived at her car, he opened the trunk and tossed in his equipment bag. "We have about two hours," he told her, unlocking the door and waiting while she slid inside. "I'll need to be back for the awards."

"I wouldn't miss that for the world."

He climbed in behind the steering wheel and started

the engine, but before putting the car in reverse, he pulled out his cell phone. "I'd better let Bridey know we won't be joining them until later."

Quickly punching in the numbers, he waited for his aunt to answer and then explained that he and Jules were going to get something to eat and would be back at the arena in time for the awards.

"She didn't mind, did she?" Jules asked when he'd finished the call and started to back the car out.

"Bridey understands" was all he said. He had no doubt his aunt was aware of his feelings for Jules, and she wouldn't make a big deal out of them wanting to spend some time alone together.

Taking Jules's hand, he laced his fingers with hers and tempered the natural urge to speed them on their way. He wouldn't rush this. He'd let her take the lead and he'd follow wherever it took them.

He parked in the space in front of his room and turned off the engine, reminding himself again to take it slow. He opened his door, then got out and waited for her to join him. He took her hand and walked her to the door of his room. Before he put the key in the lock, he turned to her. "Did you want to get something to eat first? A drink, maybe?"

Jules laughed and the sexy sound sent waves of pleasure through him. "Tanner," she said, "are you trying to stall?"

It was his turn to laugh. "Not on your life, darlin'. Just trying to be a gentleman."

"If I recall, this was my idea, so you've already been a gentleman."

He fumbled the key into the lock and finally managed to open the door. Inside the room, she slipped her hands between them and started on his shirt buttons. They popped open at her touch. A strangled groan rose in his throat when she laid her palm on his bared chest.

"You're gettin' ahead of me, darlin'," he murmured as she slid the shirt from his shoulders and arms. A tremor ran through him when she pressed her lips to the base of his throat. Backing her up, he settled her on the edge of the bed, tossing both his hat and hers to a chair. Then he toed off his boots.

Kneeling in front of her, he removed hers, then reached up and, one by one, undid the buttons of her vest, revealing nothing but ivory skin beneath. No bra.

He stood, pulling her to her feet, and she reached for his silver buckle. "Uh-uh, me first," he whispered.

Inch by inch, he relieved her of her vest, his gaze on the smooth, soft skin his fingers skimmed. The slower he went, the faster his heart beat and the faster he breathed.

He dropped the vest on the floor beside them, wanting to touch what he'd revealed, but needing to prolong the moment. His gaze on her breasts, he slid his knuckles down her stomach until he reached her buckle. He pulled it open, slipped the button from the buttonhole of her jeans and slowly guided the zipper down. Without waiting she did the same with his, but didn't touch him.

Pulling her jeans down her hips until they were completely off, he slipped a fingertip under the edge of her lacy panties. She responded by hooking her thumbs in the waistband of his jeans and pulling them down, along with his briefs. Kicking them off, he stood before her.

"You're gettin' ahead of me again, darlin'," he said, grinning. "We have all ni—" He sucked in a breath when she touched him. Regaining only a part of the control he lost, he slid her panties down until they dropped at her feet, then eased her onto the bed.

"I was going to say we have all night." His voice was a rasp.

"But we don't," she said.

Kissing his way across her lips and back again, his tongue slid in, touched hers, and she responded.

Beneath him, a tremor vibrated through her, and his control slipped another notch. Moving her farther onto the bed, he placed her against the pillows. He wanted her under him, around him.

With patience, he pressed into her. "Jules?" he asked, stopping. "Are you…? You've been with other men, right?"

She sighed. "It's just been a long time." She opened her eyes to gaze into his. Deep dark emerald blazed into him.

Sweat broke out on his body. *A long time?* He took a deep breath and slowly sank into her, their gazes locked. Moving carefully, he waited until she caught up with him, the rhythm of their bodies matching.

Her eyes darkened even more before he joined their lips and lost himself in the feel of her. When her breathing accelerated and he felt her tense, he increased his rhythm until she trembled beneath him, tightening and pulling him up and over the edge with her. Chanting her name, he poured himself, body and heart, into her.

He held her against him later, after their heartbeats had slowed, and her breath whispered against his skin. He thought she'd fallen asleep.

"Don't leave me, Tanner."

"Not until we have to leave for the arena," he promised.

He pulled her on top of him, and his body responded to the scattered kisses she placed across his chest.

"Darlin'—" His breath caught in his chest as her kisses dropped lower, and he wondered how he'd find a way to live after the novelty of this cowboy wore off for her. How long could he keep her with him before she left him like all the others had?

# Chapter Nine

Tanner hadn't bothered to rub salt in Rowdy's wounds when he earned enough points in Coffeyville to qualify for Nationals. Rowdy could see for himself how good Jules was for him. He'd never ridden better. As long as he could place in the top three for the remainder of the season, he'd be in Las Vegas for National Finals Rodeo in December.

He was definitely riding on a high, especially after the night before with Jules. To say he was struck speechless was an understatement, but not speechless enough to say no. Not crazy enough, either. Still, he had the feeling time was running out. He just couldn't put his finger on why he felt this way.

They'd left Coffeyville early in the morning for the drive back to the ranch. Jules planned to stay until evening, and Tanner had just spent two hours trying to catch up on ranch paperwork. He hadn't seen her since breakfast that morning, but he knew she'd left the house with Shawn and a promise to spend all afternoon with only Tanner.

In the horse barn, while he waited for Jules to return with Shawn, Tanner planned to saddle his gentlest mare and coax Jules into mounting the placid animal. One way or another, he'd get her begging to ride more.

As he reached for the saddle blanket draped across the stall gate, he heard her voice.

"You may never find him, Shawn."

From his vantage point, Tanner could see her walking into the dimly lit interior of the barn. He'd been wondering what Jules and Shawn had been discussing yesterday with their heads together. He had hoped it was Jules persuading Shawn to cool it with his latest group of friends and abide by house rules.

Curious, and not wanting his presence known yet, he stepped back into the corner of the stall.

"I still have to try," Shawn answered, a stubborn tone creeping into his voice. "I know Uncle Tanner thinks I'm going to take off like my dad did, but I won't unless it's the only way to find him."

Surprised by Shawn's revelation, Tanner remained silent and listened. By the sounds of their voices and movements, he could tell they'd stopped near the front of the barn.

"I thought I found him in Dodge City," Shawn went on, "but he disappeared before I could get to him." His voice took on an excited quality. "I know he's involved in rodeo somehow."

"So that's where you disappeared to that night," Jules gently scolded. "You scared me to death, Shawn. I was responsible for you while Tanner rode. When I couldn't find you, I was frantic."

"You thought I'd run off." His tone was belligerent.

"I didn't know," she said. "The next time you think you see your dad, you let me know, okay? Maybe I can help."

"You mean you would?"

"Of course. Just don't take off like that again."

Tanner wasn't sure whether to be angry or hurt. What could his nephew do to find Tucker when several expensive and thorough private detectives hadn't been able to find him? Tanner missed his brother and wished he'd been there to raise Shawn, but he hadn't been. Tucker had never even called to ask about his own flesh and blood. Because of that, Tanner couldn't forgive him, but he hoped that if Tucker was ever found, amends could be made.

The soft whinny of a horse and the sound of the barn door scooting open, followed by the soft clip-clop of hooves told him they'd taken out a horse. Standing, he replaced the blanket and left the stall, then slipped out of the barn through a little-used side door. He rounded the corner of the barn and stopped in his tracks.

Jules sat astride a chestnut gelding, looking as if she'd been born on it. One hand held the reins, the other rested on her thigh.

Tanner's heart swelled at her courage. "I'll be damned."

Jules jumped at the sound of his voice, yanking the reins. The horse beneath her lurched and sidestepped. Tanner hurried to calm the animal, but Jules brought him under control with soft words and a pat.

She smiled down at Tanner. "We wanted to surprise you."

He knuckled his hat back for a better view of her, and then jammed his hands in his pockets to keep from reaching up to drag her into his arms. He'd never felt prouder of anyone. "You sure did that, darlin'."

Her smile lit an already sunny day to blinding brilliance. He'd been all too aware of her fear of riding again, had felt it when he'd held her on his own horse. But she'd overcome it without help from him. Words of admiration escaped him, leaving him speechless.

Shawn approached, leading his own horse. "She's been working on it while you were holed up in your office. She caught on quick, once she realized it was like riding a bike, and relaxed."

Tanner nodded, staring up at her. He knew his grin had to look foolish, but he couldn't stop. It was a miracle. "Shawn," he said without breaking his gaze with Jules, "would you mind if I took Jules for a ride?"

"No, I guess not."

Tanner laid his hand on her thigh. "Just let me get my horse."

He'd never saddled a horse so fast in his life. Before leaving the barn, he grabbed two large blankets from a cabinet. He knew just where to ride. In the south pasture, a creek ran through his land. It had been a haven in times of joy and sorrow. He'd spent time there as a young child when his mother returned after the first time she'd disappeared, nearly getting lost on his way back home. He'd gone again when she'd run off the second time, never to return. When he won his first event, he'd spent the next afternoon quietly celebrating his triumph with a six-pack of stolen beer. The spot had served its soothing purpose after his dad's death, and held his frustration and anger at himself when Tucker had gone away. He'd never taken a living soul with him, never shared its special solitude. He wanted Jules to see it.

"Where are we going?" she asked as they rode through the pasture gate.

"My place."

The sound of her soft laughter caught on the light breeze. "We're at your place."

His throat thickened with strange new feelings. "Different place."

They rode on in silence, side by side. Her ease and assurance on the gelding surprised him even more. The horse she was on wasn't as gentle as the one he would have chosen for her, but she didn't seem to have a problem handling it. For someone who'd been paralyzed with fear at just the *idea* of riding, her courage beat his, hands down.

"Think you can keep up?" he asked when they approached a hill.

Without a shred of doubt in her eyes, she smiled at him. "Just try me."

He gave his horse a kick and urged it into a canter. Jules did the same, and they soon reached the crest of the hill. He reined in his mount and she joined him to look below where the creak ran, surrounded by leafy, gnarled tress along its banks.

"It's beautiful," she whispered, gazing at the scene.

"Yep." His attention was on her. He knew the landscape by heart. And it didn't compare to her.

She turned to him. "Can we go down there?"

"That's exactly where we're going." He urged his horse forward and let Jules ride a little ahead of him. The sight of her in a place that meant so much to him took his breath away. He watched her body move naturally with each step of her horse. Her long, blond braid swayed from side to side, and her hips moved in a gentle, seductive rhythm, reminding him of their time together the night before.

When he called to her to pull up and stop, she almost looked disappointed, but her warm smile told him nothing today would do that. He dismounted quickly and held out his arms. She leaned down, and he brought her off the horse and set her on her feet. Without a word, he reached for the blanket and spread it under the tree on the soft grass. He pulled her down onto it with him and proceeded to slowly unbutton her top.

"This is a special place," she said, looking around.

Her husky voice floated through him, creating heat in its wake. "If it wasn't before, it sure is now, darlin'," he whispered.

They made slow, lazy love under the green-leafed canopy, the sun peeking through in dapples of diamond lights. Their breathing mingled with the whispers of the late-summer breeze, fading into the hushed quiet of the countryside.

Afterward he pulled her on top of him, wanting only to relish the scent of her until the sun set and darkness surrounded them. But there were things to do back at the ranch, and he didn't want to have to deal with Rowdy's grumbling if those things didn't get done.

"We'll have to come here more often," he whispered. "At least until the snow comes."

Her laugh was soft. "That sounds more promising than practical. We could freeze out here before the first snowflake falls."

"We'll manage somehow." He could only hope, but if things worked the way they always had before, she'd be gone well before the first snowfall. And he didn't know how to prevent that. He knew he loved her. The realization had sneaked up on him. The first time he'd thought of the word love in relation to her, it hadn't surprised him. He hadn't bothered to deny it. It felt too right.

He knew she cared for him, too. But even though she drove down each weekend to watch him compete, he suspected she didn't understand his need to ride.

Not that he was any better. He had yet to overcome his unwillingness to take a chance on love. He had no doubt the pain would be unbearable when she walked away, even greater than losing his parents and brother. All he could do now was keep her with him as long as he could.

She rolled onto her back on the blanket and sighed. "It's so beautiful and peaceful here anything seems possible."

Turning onto his side to watch her, he propped up his head on his elbow. "Like what, darlin'?"

"Oh, I don't know. Hopes. Dreams. Goals." She turned to face him. "You have goals, don't you?"

Feeling a chill, he reached for the other blanket and pulled it over them. "Sure."

"Want to share?" she asked, grinning.

He hesitated for a moment, wondering if she would judge him or if his answer might drive her away sooner. But if that happened, it happened. He wouldn't give up his dreams for anyone. Put them on hold if it was necessary, yes, but never give up.

With no reason not to tell her, he did. "Nobody in my family has ever made it to National Finals Rodeo."

"That's the big one, right?"

"Biggest in the country," he said. "Only the best compete."

"And you want to be one of them."

"I don't reckon I'd win, not the first time there, anyway." Since he was a kid, competing in the Nationals had been a dream. When he grew up, it became a goal. And now he was almost there. He felt confident he could go all the way and ride with the best of the best, but he wasn't sure he could leave it until he won the championship buckle.

"I'm getting older," he went on, "and I don't know how long my body will hold out. If I don't make it this time or even the next, I'll know when it's time to quit. I'm just not ready to do that. Not yet. But the time will come. And there are other things in life, too, that come into play. It won't be long until Shawn is competing on a regular basis. I want to be there to see that, not off doing *my* thing."

She touched his cheek with her fingers, a sweet smile on her face. "You're a good man, Tanner."

"What about you?" he asked. "What are your goals and dreams?"

A faraway look, as if she was gazing into the distance, filled her eyes. "When I was a little girl, I wanted to be a world-class jumper. That's all I thought about, day and night. But that ended when I was twelve. The time I spent in the hospital made me see the world as it really was. Not everyone was as fortunate as I was. Some of the others there didn't even know their parents or their parents never bothered to visit, while mine were there every day, cheering each little improvement I made."

"Everyone is dealt a different hand. You can't blame yourself for what you've had," he said.

"I know that, but after those months in the hospital and in speech therapy, I understood what my parents meant when they said there were many people of all ages who didn't have the advantages I had. And that's when I knew I wanted to help."

"And you decided to become a lawyer," he finished.

"Well, not exactly," she said, laughing. "I was half-way through high school when I made that decision, and after doing a lot of research, too."

"You don't take anything lightly, do you."

"The law is complicated," she answered with a sigh. "And now that I've been a part of it, I see there are other and maybe better ways I can help. That's why I became a court advocate."

"You knew the ins and outs of the court system, so you had an advantage."

"Exactly." Her grin brightened an already sunny day. "See how quick you are?" she teased.

"And here you thought I was just another dumb cowboy," he countered, tucking a stray lock of hair behind her ear.

Leaning closer, she kissed him. "I never once thought you were dumb."

"So you're back with the advocacy and lawyer things now that your vacation is over."

"Not exactly," she said, turning her head away.

With his finger, he turned it back. "How so?"

She shook her head. "With the lawyer thing, yes, I'm back at that. As for the advocacy…"

"What?"

"There's been a problem. My latest, a boy about Shawn's age, was in foster care. He ran away. I was trying to get the court to allow him to go back to living with his mother. She's straightened out her life and can provide him with a loving and stable home. But his running away has made it difficult to get the court to agree."

"I guess you can't help all of them."

"I wish I could."

They were both quiet for a moment. Words came drifting back to Tanner. Something his mother had said to him before she left the second time. *Reach for the moon and land among the stars.* He knew what his moon was. It was and always had been to win the bronc-riding championship at the Nationals. If he could just make it to compete—once—that was his star.

"I remember Sally telling me something," he told Jules, and repeated the saying for her. "What's your moon, darlin'?"

"That's easy," she said, smiling. "I want to help troubled children in a much bigger way. I've been taking more college courses so I'll have the degrees and the knowledge I need to do that."

"What kind of bigger way?"

"I'd have a place for them, like a ranch, maybe, where there would be caring professionals and they'd feel accepted."

"That's the most unselfish dream I've ever heard, darlin'. I think you'll make it just fine." He meant every word, but it also revealed how different their goals were. Like night and day. All he could do was hope that somehow they could find a way to overcome those differences. But he knew there were no guarantees where love was concerned. He was proof of that. He wouldn't get his hopes up, but he wouldn't give up yet, either.

Looking into the green depths of her eyes, he spoke slowly, careful not to tell her more than he could risk. "We have something special, darlin', just like my place here. I don't know where this is going. I'm afraid to ask. Things like this don't work out for me. My only successes have been on this ranch and on the backs of broncs."

She pressed her fingers to his lips. "You have more than that. Look at Shawn. Look at what you've done for me." A smile turned up the corners of her mouth, tempting him to kiss her again.

He thought of how she'd touched his heart with her courage and caring. If only he could do the same for her. "I can't make promises, Jules," he said simply. "One day at a time is all I can offer right now. Is it enough?"

"Yes," she whispered.

For the moment, that *was* enough.

TANNER CLIMBED over the wooden planks into the chute at the Will Rogers Memorial Rodeo in Vinita, Oklahoma, the following Friday, ready to do his best. Just his luck, he'd drawn Copenhagen, the most unpredictable of the stock, for this ride. It could mean a good score if he stayed on for the eight seconds and his spurring was good. If it all came together, he could be sitting in the top spot. The others would have to work to catch him.

He felt confident, despite his draw. A peacefulness had settled on him after the time he and Jules had spent at his place by the creek almost a week before. She'd stayed for dinner that night, and afterward, they'd all retired outside to the porch, where a laziness in the air muted the anticipation of the next weekend. He'd claimed the porch swing, pulling Jules down next to him. Her scent filled him, reminding him of wildflowers and loving. She settled against him in the dark, and if anyone thought it strange, they hadn't commented. Not even Rowdy.

Before he'd released her for the night, before she started for home, he'd kissed her at her car. He'd done it with all the promise in his heart that he couldn't put into words. In return, he'd felt her love touch his soul.

When they'd parted company before this ride, she'd wished him luck as always, her hand resting in his for a lingering moment. Now, poised above one of the toughest broncs he'd ridden over the circuit season, he forced the vision from his mind. Concentration could be his only friend. He'd ride this brute until the horn blew. For himself. For his dad. For Jules.

He checked his spurs and rigging, double-checking his grip and the feel. His heart had stopped hammering and slowed to a hard thud. Mindless of everything around him, he breathed slowly until he felt right. Mounted on the bronc's back, his concentration focused on the ride, the horse and his own body, he readied to mark out and signaled for the chute to open.

"IF HE CAN HOLD on until the horn, he'll be sitting good in the standings."

Jules turned to find Dusty settling in the seat behind her, his slow drawl comforting. She offered him a nervous smile before turning back to watch Tanner climb into the chute. Her hands clenched between her denim-clad knees, she jumped when Dusty laid his hand on her shoulder.

"He'll do fine," he told her, his confidence in his friend evident in his tone. "I saw him a few minutes ago and there was no doubt about his determination. You could see it in his eyes."

"And his edge?" She'd heard Rowdy talk often enough about it.

"Never saw him so cool."

She could only pray Dusty was right. Beside her, Bridey patted her arm. "It won't be long now. And then we can go out and celebrate."

"He's taking forever," Jules whispered.

"He's just getting his grip right," Dusty answered, "and positioning himself to mark out."

"Mark out?"

"He has to have both spurs touching the horse's shoulders until the horse's feet hit the ground after he's out of the chute."

"I never noticed," she said, thinking of the rides she'd seen in the past few weeks.

"Watch closely," Dusty continued. "When the bronc bucks, Tanner will pull his knees up and roll his spurs up the horse's shoulders. Then when the horse goes down again, Tanner'll straighten his legs, with his spurs going over the point of the horse's shoulders, ready for the next jump."

"So I guess there's more to it than just staying on the horse," Jules said.

Shawn leaned forward. "A lot more. Each rider is judged on his marking. Bareback bronc riding is the toughest sport in rodeo."

"And has the most injuries," Dusty added.

She looked at him, concerned now more than ever. "I wish you hadn't told me that."

Dusty shook his head and looked out at the arena. Jules wasn't sure what to make of the head shake. Was it because, like Rowdy, he thought she wasn't good for Tanner?

"You need to know these things, Jules," he finally

said. "We all play down the dangers. Take my cracked ribs and all the concussions I've had riding bulls, for instance. But that doesn't mean you shouldn't be knowledgeable. This way you'll know what you're facing and what *not* to worry about. Tanner's a tough guy. Big for a bronc rider, but he's in great shape. He'll do okay, believe me. He's been riding broncs since he was a little guy."

She nodded, keeping her eyes on the chute. There were dangers in everything. Even show-jumping, as she knew from experience. She had known that as well as Tanner knew the dangers of his own chosen sport.

His black hat and shoulders were visible above the chute, but little more. The arena was big, and she'd purposely chosen seats far from the chutes. Too close, and she'd hear every breath the horse took, hear the hooves beat the dirt, see the pain on Tanner's face.

Oblivious to the announcer's voice, she waited, forcing herself to relax and not worry. Tanner raised his arm high, nodded and the chute opened.

*Eight seconds. Eight long seconds.*

Copenhagen shot out with Tanner high atop him. Jules watched, unable to take her eyes off the man and horse. Eight seconds seemed like an eternity.

"That's it!" Dusty shouted in her ear above the noise of the buzzer and the crowd.

The animal continued to buck, even after Tanner kicked loose and fell in the dirt, landing on his hands and knees. One of the pick-up men rode over. While reaching for Tanner, the cowboy dodged the hoof of the still-bucking bronc. But before the hoof hit dirt again, it connected with Tanner's head, knocking him flat.

Jules opened her mouth to scream, but nothing

came out. From behind, Dusty grabbed her shoulders. "They'll get him out," he assured her. "They'll get him out."

Seconds dragged by in slow motion. Two more cowboys ran out to join the ones on horses who were attempting to keep the bronc at bay and herd it to the corner gate. Grabbing Tanner's arms, they pulled him out of the way to safety.

Dusty helped Jules climb over her seat to stand beside him. "Come on, honey."

She barely heard him through the fog of darkness filling her mind. Her feet moved beneath her, but she wasn't aware of making them. Dusty kept his arm tightly around her, and Bridey held on to her hand, while Shawn followed. They pushed and shoved their way through a meandering crowd of people. Dusty moved people aside without an apology, and Jules didn't care. She'd been raised to act with the best of manners, but she'd have shoved her way through herself if he hadn't done it.

When she stumbled, his hold tightened. He swiped at a burly cowboy, moving him out of the way. "We're almost there, hon," he told her.

Color left her world, and everything blurred into a mass of grays. She choked on a sob and stumbled again, only to be brought up when they reached a knot of people in the way.

"The Justin Healers are taking care of him," Dusty said. "He's in good hands."

She nodded, not caring who they were, only praying they knew what to do and would do it quickly. Staring blindly at the group, she recognized a familiar figure shoving his way out of the tangle of people.

"Get her out of here," Rowdy ordered, pointing at Jules.

"Now, Rowdy—"

"Don't argue with me." Rowdy grabbed Dusty's arm and pulled him aside.

Tanner's aunt stiffened beside Jules, fiercely gripping her hand. "Bridey, it's okay," Jules said. "I know he's only concerned for Tanner." But she wanted to scream that she had the right to go to him. She loved him and he loved her. She'd never been more certain of anything.

They had no choice but to wait and watch. When the crowd moved back, she saw an ambulance, its doors wide open. Without a thought for anyone but Tanner, she elbowed her way through the crowd and watched two attendants loading a stretcher into the back. Tanner lay unmoving on it, his black lashes standing out against his skin. He was pale under his tan. Too pale. And too still. Blood spread on a bandage on his head. An IV tube ran from under the blanket covering him to a bag in an attendant's hand.

"Tanner," she cried. But they closed the doors, cutting her off from him.

Dusty reached her side and grabbed her when her legs gave way beneath her. She went hot, then cold, and the edges of her vision began to blacken.

"Rowdy, take Bridey to the hospital with you," Dusty's voice floated to her from a distance. "Where's Shawn?"

"Right here" came the boy's voice.

"Go with them. I'll bring Jules."

"Dusty," Rowdy called, "get his bag!"

Darkness enveloped her, and then there was nothing.

JULES'S NOSE BURNED and she brushed at it, hitting something warm. She twisted her head away from the offensive, tear-wrenching smell.

"Come on, Jules," a man's voice urged her. "Open your eyes, hon."

*Dusty.* She could feel hard ground beneath her. Slowly opening her eyes, she saw him kneeling beside her.

"Good," he said. He was grinning at her, but his brown eyes were filled with concern. He helped her to a sitting position and then took her by the waist to help her to her feet. "Let's go. We need to get to the hospital."

*Tanner's hurt.*

The thought hit her like a sonic boom, its force making her stagger. "Oh, God," she moaned.

Steadying her, Dusty gripped her shoulders and bent to her level. His gaze bore into her. "Listen to me, Jules. You've got to get hold of yourself. You can't fall to pieces. It won't help you and it won't help Tanner."

Taking a deep breath, she nodded. "But Rowdy doesn't want me there. He wanted me gone." Tears filled her eyes at the thought of having to face the ranch foreman and fight him to be with Tanner.

Dusty gave her a shake. "You're wrong, Jules. He just didn't want you to see Tanner until they'd cleaned him up."

Panic stilled her heart, and she couldn't raise her voice above a rough whisper. "Is Tanner...going to be all right?"

Dusty's sigh frightened her even more. "Damn horse split his hard head open a tad. He was unconscious when they left here, but my guess is he'll be kicking and screaming to get out in no time."

Relief made her weak. He caught her once more around the waist and started to lead her away. "Wait," she said, stopping. "Tanner's bag. I remember hearing Rowdy say to bring it."

Dusty reversed their direction and pointed a few yards ahead. "It should be over there."

When they were detained by a mustached man with a notepad and pen asking questions about Tanner's career, Jules slipped away. It took one glance in the area where Dusty had pointed to identify Tanner's bag, sitting worn and forlorn against a wall. Still feeling wobbly, she bent and picked it up. Her energy had deserted her. Only fear remained. And she knew she could never go through it again.

*Chapter Ten*

Jules waited by Dusty's truck while he asked for directions to the hospital where Tanner was being transported. It didn't take long to find someone who knew and Dusty was unlocking and opening the door for her.

"Twenty minutes, maybe," he said as she climbed into the truck. "But I think I can make it quicker."

She waited as patiently as possible as he slid into the driver's seat and started the engine. "I don't care how fast you go. Just don't get stopped."

He glanced over to grin at her as he drove through the crowded parking lot. "But I have a lawyer with me. Surely you could bail me out in no time."

"I'd let the police take you, and I'd drive on to the hospital," she replied. "And how can you joke at a time like this? Tanner is on his way to the hospital with a concussion."

"Why are you thinking the worst?" he asked, pulling out onto the street.

"Because I know just how bad a head injury can be."

"And I've had more concussions than I can count." His sigh was heavy as he maneuvered through traffic.

"Look, Jules, there's no sense thinking the worst until that's what we know it is. You gotta have hope, because without it... I know Tanner's bronc riding is hard for you to deal with, and I know what happened today is the reason why. You've just been waiting for it or something like it to happen, haven't you?"

She couldn't honestly say she hadn't, but she wouldn't admit it, either.

"It was a fluke that he got hung up in the rigging and tossed on the ground like that, but it happens," Dusty continued when she didn't answer. "It's happened to him before, so don't be thinking it's your fault in some way."

She understood that Dusty was only trying to be honest with her, and she was glad he was. At this point, she needed someone who wouldn't sugarcoat things. "I've tried to be supportive. And I'm trying to be positive. It's just very difficult."

"I know you have, and I appreciate it."

"But you said—"

"Yeah, I know what I said. But I've also seen how hard you've been trying to accept his bronc riding, not just trying to *look* like you do, so maybe it doesn't apply. If it ever did." He took a breath and glanced at her briefly. "Don't tell anybody you heard me say it, but you're a good woman. Tanner's my best friend and I only want the best for him. I think he's found it with you, so don't disappoint me."

He added a smile, but Jules couldn't return it or even reply. It was too hard to think while worrying about Tanner. The future, even if only a few hours, was too far away.

"They'll probably run some tests if he hasn't gained consciousness," Dusty said. "An MRI, CT scan, what-

ever all those fancy tests are they do. By the time we get
there, they may know more. Until then, let's concentrate
on him being okay. All right?"

"All right," Jules answered, and did her best to stay
positive. It wasn't as easy as it sounded.

The rest of the ride to the hospital seemed endless, but
they finally arrived. At the Emergency admittance desk,
they were told Tanner was stable and had been moved to
a private room. After getting directions, the pair walked
through the hushed hallways, searching for the area
where they expected the others would be waiting. The
farther they went, the faster Jules's heart beat.

What if Tanner's injuries were worse than they'd been
told? What if it was her fault he'd been hurt? If he'd lost
his concentration for just one second because of her, how
would she ever face the rest of the family? How would
she face Rowdy, knowing he might have been right all
along? But worst of all, how would she face herself?

Her anxiety grew with each step. One adrenaline
rush after another made her senseless. Despite her love
for Tanner, all the ifs, ands and buts crowded her mind.
Injuries in rodeo were common. Tanner's own father had
died competing. And no matter how often she tried to
tell herself she'd get used to the savagery of the sport,
she hadn't. Her fear hadn't vanished and might never,
even though she was able to watch. She wasn't sure she
could continue this way, no matter how much she loved
Tanner. Her only hope was that he would decide he'd
had enough.

"There they are."

Dusty's voice broke into her thoughts and his footsteps quickened. She lengthened her shorter stride to

keep up, and he squeezed her hand, obviously for strength and encouragement. Dread filled her as they turned the corner and approached Tanner's family, sitting in the barren waiting area.

HIS HEAD HURT. His arm felt like a dead weight when he tried to raise it to massage the throbbing. He carefully opened his eyes. The room was unfamiliar and dark. Without moving his head, he tried to get his bearings.

*Hospital.*

His last memory was of being helped to stand after his ride, and then a blinding pain had hit him. He'd made the time. And it had been a good ride, he knew that, too. Jules would be pleased.

His eyes slowly drifted shut, and darkness descended once again.

"HOW'S HE DOING?" Dusty asked Bridey when they joined her and Shawn in the waiting room.

Jules noticed that Rowdy was missing and felt a moment of relief. She was battling enough guilt as it was, without having to face him.

Bridey looked at Jules and patted the empty space next to her on the sofa, while she answered Dusty. "They're taking him down for some tests in a few minutes. The doctor said they'd know more when they're done."

"How serious do they think it is?" Jules asked, dreading the answer she might hear as she joined Bridey on the sofa.

The older woman frowned, scooting over to make more room for Jules. "The doctor said it's hard to tell.

Tanner's still being unconscious isn't a good sign, but it might not mean anything. That's why they're doing the tests."

Shawn, who was sitting in a chair across a small table from them, leaned forward. "Dusty's the one who knows about concussions."

"Most bull riders do," Dusty replied. "Not so much with bronc riders. They have more shoulder and back problems." He turned to look at Shawn. "You keep that in mind."

Shawn fought hard to keep a smile from springing to his lips. "There's always team roping with you, Dusty."

"That there is, and we're going to get back to practicing just as soon as we can. No reason you can't be in two events."

Jules was aware of the conversation as it continued, but she wasn't hearing it. She was remembering her own accident. Before it had happened, she had never been afraid to climb on a horse—any horse. She'd known the dangers inherent in jumping, but she was a good rider—an excellent rider, according to her trainer, who'd kept pushing her to do more. She'd expected to make the jump as she rode up to it. Her horse had taken similar ones with no problem. But she'd been pushing herself for several weeks, thanks to her trainer, and was feeling the tiniest bit nervous. That was all it had taken. For whatever reason—maybe her horse had sensed she wasn't one hundred percent with him—he had decided not to take the jump. Before she had realized what was happening, she had felt herself being propelled in the air.

She knew even better than some people that there were no guarantees. A person either found something else to focus on or gave it his or her all. She had chosen to walk away. Tanner gave it his all.

Would he be like her? Even if he was all right when he regained consciousness, would he decide, as she had, that it wasn't worth it? She would never tell anyone, but she hoped he'd be ready to stop risking his life. In fact, there was a part of her that was counting on it, even though she knew it was wrong. After all, he had shown her that she didn't have to be afraid of riding. But that didn't mean she wasn't still afraid for him.

They all looked up at the sudden ruckus at the end of the long hallway. Buzzers and bells went off, and hospital personnel scattered. Even the nurse at the nurses' station left her desk and hurried away. Jules prayed it didn't have anything to do with Tanner. She knew the others were doing the same.

"Did they say 'code blue'?" Shawn asked. His voice was strained and his face starkly white.

Jules shook her head. "It isn't Tanner," she whispered, determined to stay positive.

Dusty nodded. "They'll let us know," he said, his voice not nearly as strong as it had been earlier.

The wait seemed to last forever, but in reality it was only a few minutes. The nurse returned to the desk and smiled at them, but said nothing. That little bit gave Jules hope.

Jules turned to look when she heard footsteps approaching, but her heart took a slight drop when she saw it was Rowdy.

"How's he doing?" he asked.

They all looked at one another, and Dusty finally answered, "As far as we know, he's still unconscious. They're running some tests. We're waiting on the—"

When he stopped, everyone turned. The doctor was walking their way and looked tired, but when he joined them, he smiled.

Bridey took Jules's hand and gripped it tightly and they both stood. "Do you have any news?" she asked the doctor.

He looked from one to the other before answering. "Preliminary results show no permanent damage, which is good news. There's a little swelling on the brain, but we expect that to take care of itself over time."

Relief flooded Jules. Beside her, Bridey squeezed her hand and asked, "How much time?"

"My guess would be several hours, maybe by morning, but it could be longer. Some take more time. It just depends on the patient. You're all from out of town?"

"We're here for the rodeo," Rowdy answered.

Bridey nodded. "We're from Desperation, not far from Oklahoma City."

"But you're staying here?"

"We have motel rooms not far from the arena."

"Good," the doctor said. "My suggestion is for all of you to go on back to your motel, get some rest and come back here in the morning. There's no reason for you to stay here at the hospital. Mr. O'Brien isn't in any danger. If there's any change before morning, someone will call you. Just leave your name and a number where you can be reached with the nurse."

"I'll go do that now," Dusty said, and started for the desk.

"Any questions?" the doctor asked.

Bridey shook her head. "None that I can think of. Not right now, anyway."

"If you have any later, just call and ask the nurse. She

can get in touch with me if needed." The doctor turned and left them to decide what to do next.

Dusty returned from the nurses' station. "He's in his room again, but he's still unconscious."

The frown on Rowdy's face only intensified Jules's guilt. Whether she was responsible for Tanner's accident or not, Rowdy believed she was.

"He's a tough one," Rowdy said. "He'll be fine. Up and around in no time."

Bridey patted Jules's hand. "Of course he will. The O'Briens are hardy stock."

Determined to say what needed to be said, Jules gently pulled her hand from Bridey's. Turning to Tanner's foreman, she took a deep breath. "I'm sorry, Rowdy," she whispered.

He looked at her through narrowed eyes. "Nothin' to be sorry for. Doesn't have anything to do with you. It's just one of those things that happen."

"But—"

He moved to put his arm around her. "I hope you're not blaming yourself, Jules. He's had plenty of injuries in his life, some worse than this one. None of those were anybody's fault, either. I guess it's time I admit Tanner's right. You're good for him. Haven't seen him ride better or be so happy."

Bridey joined them, smiling first at Rowdy before turning to Jules. "Why don't you go in and see him, Jules? The nurse said earlier that he was mumbling something about jewelry. I'm sure he was calling for you."

Rowdy patted her arm and stepped back. "He's a fighter, girl. He'll be telling us all what to do in no time. You go on in for a minute."

Jules nodded and walked to the door of Tanner's room. Before pushing it open, she wiped her damp palms on her jeans.

Inside, the room was dark, with only a small, dim light burning above the bed. She crept closer in silence, intent on the figure lying in the bed. His black hair and tanned face were starkly evident in their stillness on the pillow. His color had returned, and he seemed to be breathing easily. A strip of gauze was wrapped around his head to hold the bandage that peeked out at the back.

Not wanting to disturb him, she gently placed her hand on his where it lay on top of the blanket. It could have been worse, she reminded herself. The injury wasn't as severe as they'd feared. But she also knew that anything could have happened. He could very well be dead, instead of injured.

They could all rest easy now, but she knew she wouldn't. Not until Tanner was conscious and sitting up in that bed. Or better yet, out of the hospital completely and back with his family on the ranch.

Dusty's warning came back to haunt her. She thought she'd made her decision, but maybe she was wrong. Maybe it would have been better if she hadn't shown up at Ponca City, before her heart had become so involved. Better for Tanner, too.

She spent a restless night, tossing and turning in her motel-room bed, trying her best not to wake Bridey in the bed beside her. All she knew for certain was that she couldn't go through watching him get hurt again, and if there was to be a future with him, his bronc riding would be an issue they would have to talk about.

TANNER SAT propped against pillows in the hospital bed, waiting for Jules. Running his hand over the new growth of beard on his face, he wished for a razor. But the doctor had assured him he'd be going home later in the day. A shave could wait.

He'd awakened to a wan sunrise, his room bathed in the dusky light from the windows. His first thought had been of Jules. When the nurse came to check on him later, he'd asked for her, only to be told she and the others had gone for breakfast. Disappointed, he'd grumbled at the nurse while she took his pulse and blood pressure. Now, left alone, he strained for sounds in the hallway outside. When he finally heard familiar voices, he waited, anxious to see them all, but especially Jules.

The door opened and she walked in. Tanner's breathing stopped at the sight of her. The thought had crossed his mind that she might have knuckled under to her fear and taken off. But she hadn't. She'd stayed.

He crooked his finger at her. "Come here, darlin'," he whispered roughly.

"Everyone is waiting to see you, but they insisted I come in first." She approached with cautious steps, and he noticed the dark circles under her eyes. Her sparkle had gone, and she looked worn-out, but she was still the most beautiful woman in the world.

"They can wait a little longer." He patted the bed. "Closer, darlin'. I want to be able to touch you."

With the same caution, she perched on the edge of the bed. Distress and worry filled her eyes. "How's your head?" she asked.

"I can't feel a thing, now that you're here." He stroked

her cheek with the back of his hand, drinking in the feel of her skin. She smiled, but it didn't stop the worry that formed in his mind. "Are you okay?"

A small smile lifted her frown, but she broke eye contact. "Just tired. It was a long night for all of us."

"Sorry, darlin'. I didn't mean to worry you." Her face was unreadable. Slipping an arm around her waist, he pulled her closer. "I could sure use a kiss."

Complying, she gently pressed her mouth to his. He felt a reticence in the kiss and guessed she was worried she might hurt him. His thumping head forgotten, he kissed her more surely.

When he finally released her, her face was flushed, her lips slightly swollen, and her eyes had darkened to a deep forest green. If only his head didn't hurt, he'd be out of bed and they'd be on their way to someplace more private.

"Everyone is eager to see you," she said as she eased away and moved off the bed.

He held on to her hand, reluctant to let go for any reason. "You're the one I want right now, darlin'."

Slipping out of his grasp, she smiled. "They've been as worried as I have, Tanner."

She ducked out the door before he could answer. Her concern for his family only increased his love for her. But damn! He'd wanted to be alone with her for just a little longer.

Shawn and Bridey entered the room first, and Rowdy and Dusty followed, with Jules scooting in last. Their voices were hushed at first, but soon they'd all gathered around his bed, all talking at once. Tanner tried to sort through each of their versions of his ride.

"You sure got your daddy's talent," Rowdy told him when quiet descended again.

"For getting thrown and stomped, too, it seems," Tanner answered wryly, fingering the gauze on his head. "But I got lucky. I know now just how lucky." He looked from his foreman to Jules, who stood away from the group. Having her there and knowing she hadn't run off only confirmed that he'd hit the best lucky streak of his life when he'd met her. He needed some time alone with her. He needed to tell her how much she meant to him. He needed to tell her he loved her and wanted a future with her.

She smiled at him. "Why don't I let you all have some time together?"

"Don't run off, darlin'," he told her as she turned to leave. "They'll be letting me out of here in a few hours, and we'll go home." The sound of the word warmed his heart. He turned to Dusty. "You planning to be in San José next weekend?"

Dusty patted his side. "These old ribs are all healed up. I wouldn't miss it for the world. What about you?"

"I'll be in Nebraska."

"The Oregon Trail Rodeo? That's a good one."

Out of the corner of his eye Tanner saw the look on Jules's face. She stood with her back to the door, her eyes on him.

"Jules?" he asked, not sure what was wrong.

"You can't be serious about riding next weekend, Tanner."

"Of course I am, darlin'."

The others stepped away from the bed, and he had a clear view of her. The horror in her eyes baffled him, and when she spoke, her voice was strained. "You have a concussion and stitches in your head, and you're going to ride again? Isn't nearly getting yourself killed enough for you?"

Tanner blinked, then stared at her. "You fall off a horse, you get right back on."

Her chin went up and her words were ice-coated. "You didn't fall off a horse. You were kicked by one. Apparently it did more damage than they thought."

He gripped the edge of the blanket in his hands. Anger and fear took over, and he prayed he could keep his voice from shaking. "Jules, darlin', I'm fine. This isn't any kind of setback. It's nothing that'll stop me from riding again. I'll be fine in a week. I don't have a choice. As it is, this little mishap has probably put me behind in the standings."

"And that's what's important to you? The *standings?*"

"It's what's always been important, darlin'. You know that." It was as if his family had disappeared, and all he could see was Jules. Somehow he had to make her understand. "I'm going to Finals this year. And if something happens and I don't make the cut, I'll try again next year, and the next, until I do." He took a deep, shuddering breath. "And I want you with me."

Her head moved slowly back and forth. "I...I can't, Tanner," she whispered loudly enough for him to catch her words. "I just can't watch you, knowing the next time you might be hurt worse. Or killed." Spinning around, she threw open the door and ran from the room.

No one moved or said anything, until Dusty touched his shoulder. "She'll be okay. The last couple of days have been hard on her, but she'll be back."

Tanner stared at the spot where she had been, not believing what had just happened. Unable to stand it any longer, he closed his eyes against the stinging sensation in them. "Don't count on it."

# *Chapter Eleven*

Jules balanced a box of personal belongings from her office and fought her key into the lock of her apartment. She could hear the phone ringing inside, but her fingers were all thumbs and nothing was going right. Finally she felt the click of the tumblers and nearly fell inside when the door swung open. Setting the box on the floor and nudging the door shut with her hip, she heard the last of her outgoing message and then Beth's voice.

"Jules, if you're there, pick up the phone."

Jules kicked off her wet shoes at the same time she lunged for the phone.

"Okay," Beth said, "if you're not there—"

"Beth? I'm here. Hang on a minute." Jules cradled the phone between her neck and shoulder. Her suit jacket, damp from the rainy day, clung to her as she tried to remove it. She put the phone down and peeled the sticking garments from her body, stripping down to her slip.

"...are you doing?" Beth was saying when Jules had picked up the phone again and curled up on her sofa.

"I just walked in the door when the answering

machine picked up. It's pouring rain out there and I'm a soaking mess."

"Do you want to call me back? I can wait until you get changed."

"No need for that. I'm fine."

"Did you get your packing done?"

Jules shivered and grabbed the fuzzy blue throw from the back of the sofa, covering herself and tucking her feet beneath her. She was ready for a long chat. It had been weeks since she had last talked to her best friend. "The office is empty and the movers have taken everything to storage."

"You've certainly been busy since we talked the last time."

"Busier than I've ever been, but I'm loving it." Jules knew Beth hadn't called to talk about the closing of her law office. After she'd called Beth on her return from Vinita and told her about Tanner's accident and how she'd been unable to deal with it, the few times Beth had called, Jules had refused to talk about it anymore. She was certain Beth wouldn't let go of it, and it had to be what was on her mind this time. It had been five weeks since she'd left Tanner at the hospital, and although she missed him terribly, she wasn't ready to revisit the subject.

"My courses are more interesting than I'd imagined," she continued, keeping the subject as far from Tanner as possible.

"Jules—"

"We're moving along with Joey's case, too. It looks promising," she rushed on, hoping Beth would take the hint. "I'm really hopeful the court will place him back with his mother."

"Jules—"

"I can't tell you how helpful my law experience is. And not only am I continuing work with Joey, I'm working with another child, too. It all means I don't have a lot of spare time, but—"

"Jules, I was out at the ranch yesterday."

Squeezing her eyes shut, Jules's heart skipped a beat. When would she ever get over him? "How is everyone?" she managed to ask.

Beth's exasperation showed in her sigh. "Can't you even ask about Tanner?"

Jules took a deep breath. For the first couple of weeks after she'd left him, she'd been prepared for a call from Tanner or even a visit and been ready to stand firm about her decision. But she hadn't seen or heard from him and tried desperately not to wonder why. It was over. There was nothing good in thinking about something that would never be.

"How does he look?" she asked, knowing she shouldn't.

"Well, he looked a little funny for a while with that spot where they shaved the back of his head, but—"

"Beth, you know what I mean." Now that Beth had opened up the subject like an old wound, Jules needed to hear it all.

Silence greeted her from the other end of the line. She felt like screaming before her friend spoke again.

"Anybody looking at him would see the same Tanner, I guess. He doesn't seem to be suffering any repercussions from the accident."

"I'm glad," Jules answered with a sigh of relief. She'd worried herself sick that something might have happened that they hadn't foreseen. The possibility of vision problems or memory loss had crossed her mind more than once.

"Don't be too glad," Beth replied. "That's only what somebody who didn't know him would think. But I know him. He isn't unaffected by this, Jules. One look in his eyes and it's plain to see what it's done to him."

Jules fought back memories, not willing to admit how much she missed him. "He'll get over it," she whispered.

"He's like a lost little boy," Beth went on. "It's as if he lost his soul."

Jules wanted to tell her that he wasn't the only one who'd lost something, but she didn't want Beth to remind her that it was her own fault if she hurt. "Give him time. He hasn't contacted me, so obviously I wasn't as important to him as you think I was."

"His riding suffered."

Guilt hit Jules like a sledgehammer, but she refused to give in. "I'm sorry."

"Are you?"

"Of course I am!" Taking a deep breath to calm herself, Jules knew it was time she was honest, not only with Beth, but with herself. "I know that my fear is what forced me to leave, but I can't deal with Tanner's riding, Beth. I just can't."

"How hard have you tried?"

"I've spoken with a therapist," Jules admitted.

"That's it?"

"I'm working on it, Beth, but even once I conquer that, if I ever do, there are still the differences between us." Tears threatened and her throat closed around her words. "I'm moving on, Beth. I've left my law practice behind. I'm going after my dreams."

On the other end of the connection, she heard Beth's snort. "And I guess Tanner doesn't fit in those dreams."

Jules closed her eyes, but Tanner's face floated through her mind. "No more than I fit into his."

For a moment there was silence. "He's caught up with the leader, and we're all convinced he'll be going to Las Vegas to National Finals," Beth answered. "One more win is all he needs."

Jules had admitted to herself that she had been foolish to think Tanner would quit because of a concussion and a few stitches, or because of her. He'd been born to ride broncs. He might have loved her, might still, but rodeo had been his life for too long. How could she have ever dared think he might give it up just because she couldn't deal with it?

"Jules, he loves you," Beth said, interrupting her thoughts. "Everybody knows it. Isn't there some way you can handle his riding for a while? He's so close. He needs you."

"No, Beth, I can't. I thought I could. I really did. I tried. But when I saw that hoof come down on him, I thought I'd lost him. And when he told me he planned to continue to ride, I knew I couldn't go through it again." She wiped the tears from her cheeks with the back of her hand. "Please understand that."

Beth's sniff traveled the distance between them. "I do. I just wish it didn't have to be this way. I love you both, and it hurts to see the two of you apart. You belong together."

"We're too different."

"That's why you're perfect for each other. I see how much you've changed since you met him."

"Yes, he changed me," Jules admitted. "But I can't become the woman he needs. A woman who doesn't die a little each time he climbs on the back of a bucking bronc."

JULES STOOD at the window, staring without seeing the gray November evening. The day had been more than depressing. When she had returned to Wichita after leaving Tanner in Vinita, she had been reassigned to Joey Martin's case. As court advocate for the boy, it was her responsibility to speak for him, and she was completely convinced he should be with his mother. The hearing date had been postponed several times, but it had finally been held that afternoon. The judge had ordered Joey to remain in foster care for at least three more months, if not longer. It was the worst thing that could happen to the boy, but there was nothing she could do or change. She felt completely incompetent, even more than she had when she'd gone to stay in Desperation to help with Beth's wedding.

Raindrops slid forlornly down the glass, joining others on their slow journey until, together, they fell out of sight. The evening offered the same gloom she felt.

*Lonely.* The word whispered through her mind but didn't come close to conveying the emptiness she felt. Nearly three months had passed since she'd walked out of Tanner's hospital room and his life, and the pain had finally been replaced by numbness. She had closed her law office almost two months ago and focused on Joey, making him all that mattered. But now nothing did. Even her dream seemed distant. If she couldn't help

Joey, she couldn't help herself. Her future stretched ahead of her, and there was nothing there but loneliness.

Drawing a trembling breath, she turned away, determined to change her mood. In her bedroom, her melancholy seeped through her defenses, chilling her, and she shivered. Slipping out of the suit she'd worn for court, she kicked off her shoes and pulled on a pair of jeans, a fleece sweatshirt and bulky wool socks.

She padded to the kitchen, feeling warmer on the outside, but still raw on the inside. Memories continued to pound at her, but she pushed them aside as she automatically fixed herself a cup of hot tea. When it was ready, she took the steaming, earthenware mug to the living room and set it on the end table, ready to sink onto the sofa and indulge herself.

The incessant buzzing of the doorbell interrupted her. During one of their phone calls, Beth had mentioned stopping by and had included a suggestion of a movie. But Jules didn't feel up to going out, even though she knew it would probably do her good.

"Come on in," she said morosely, swinging the door open—only to stop, stunned.

Shifting from one foot to the other was Shawn O'Brien. He looked down, avoiding eye contact. "I need to talk to you."

She peered behind him into the hallway. "Are you alone?"

He nodded and glanced up, sheepishly. "Is it okay?"

"Of course it's okay." She took his hand and drew him inside. Gesturing toward one end of the sofa, she curled up in the opposite end and waited for him to sit. "How did you get here?"

Shawn took the seat she indicated and continued to avoid looking directly at her. "I drove."

"You drove." She knew he only had a restricted license. She also knew neither Tanner nor Rowdy would have given him permission to make the three-and-a-half-hour drive alone to Wichita. "Did someone come with you, Shawn?"

He shook his head, his gaze on the floor near his feet. "No, I just got in the old ranch pickup and drove."

Her first thought was that he'd run away. Tanner didn't need this. Tanner didn't deserve it. She felt a small amount of alarm, but knew better than to let Shawn see it. Working with troubled teens had taught her to stay calm and get the facts before reacting.

"So nobody knows you're here?" she asked.

"Nope." He glanced at her, his eyes hard with stubborn determination.

"Shawn, have you and your uncle had a disagreement?"

"I'm mad at him." He hesitated before giving her an accusing glare. "And you."

"Me?" Stunned, Jules shifted on the sofa.

"Why'd you run off?" he demanded. "Everything was finally getting good. You rode a horse like you used to and promised to help me find my dad. And Uncle Tanner was doing good, too." Eyes suddenly alight, he rushed on, "He has enough points to go to Finals. And he's been really different since he met you." His smile disappeared. "At least he was. Bridey said before we went to Vinita that she'd never seen him so happy and easygoing. And Rowdy said he'd never ridden that good. Not ever. And he's okay, you know. So can't you come back?"

Unable to speak, she shook her head. Shawn's face

crumpled, breaking her already aching heart. "I'm sorry, Shawn, I just can't," she whispered.

His jaw hardened, reminding her of his uncle. "Why not?" he demanded, and then shook his head. "I don't understand any of this."

Jules forced back the tears that threatened. She didn't want Shawn to see her cry, didn't want to hurt him any more than she had wanted to hurt Tanner. She considered lying, but Shawn would catch on someday if he didn't immediately. She didn't want him to hate her, but she had to tell him the truth.

Digging her nails into her palms, she told him what she could. "It scares me, Shawn. I just can't watch him ride those broncs."

"But you did!" he said, leaning toward her. "You went to all those rodeos and sat there and watched. I know it bothered you, but you did it."

Jules took a deep breath and wondered what she could say to make him understand. "Yes, I did. But when I saw that horse's hooves come down on him, I just…" She closed her eyes, willing herself to go on. "I can't, Shawn. I just can't. It's more than I can take."

"That's nuts," he said. "You're one of the bravest people I know, Jules. It took a lot of guts to get on that horse, but you did. I know how scared you were. If you can do that, you can do anything."

She stood, turning her back to him so he wouldn't see the tears she could no longer stop. "It isn't the same thing, Shawn," she managed to say with only the slightest hint of how she'd begun to fall apart. "You'll understand it someday. Right now you'll have to take my word for it."

When he didn't answer, she turned back. He still sat on the sofa, but now with his arms spread across the back, one boot propped on his knee and a stubborn glint in his eyes.

"We need to let your folks know where you are," she told him as she reached for the phone.

"Go ahead, but tell them I may not be back for a while."

Her finger froze on the button, and she jerked her hand up to stare at him. "Excuse me?"

"I'm not going to leave until you come with me." His voice held the stubborn quality she knew so well.

"You can't do that."

He glared at her, his eyes a steely gray. "Watch me."

Jules wasn't sure what to do, but she knew his family would be worrying about him soon, if they weren't already. Dialing the number she'd never meant to memorize, she held her breath and waited for someone to answer.

*Please don't let it be Tanner.*

"Rocking O."

She let out her breath when she recognized Dusty's voice. But she detected worry in his brisk tone. "It's Jules. Shawn is here in Wichita with me."

"Thank God." His weary sigh proved his relief. "Hold on, Jules."

In the background, she heard voices, none of them Tanner's. In spite of praying he wouldn't answer, she couldn't deny she wasn't disappointed.

"You'd better send him on home, Jules."

"I will. I only called so none of you would worry."

"Thanks. We appreciate it." Silence filled the moment. "Come on back with him, Jules. It's time to put Tanner out of his misery."

"He'll get over it."

"Doubt it," Dusty replied evenly. "I don't think you have any idea what this has done to him."

"I think I have a clue."

"Nearly everybody he's ever cared about has run out on him. First his mama. And not once, but twice. His daddy up and got himself killed while looking for her. Then Tucker left. Tanner isn't going to come after you. For one thing, the man has too much pride. He'd rather live with a broken heart. So if you've been expecting him to call…"

She glanced at Shawn before answering, knowing he was listening to every word. "I don't expect anything, except that he'll go on riding broncs until he gets himself killed, too."

"If you'd just—"

"It won't work, Dusty," she said, stopping him. "I'm not going to watch him get thrown or stomped or anything else. I can't sit by calmly and watch the man I lo—" She stopped and took a breath, realizing she'd almost admitted she loved Tanner. "I can't watch a man die or be left with a broken body. You were the one who told me to get out if I couldn't take it. I should have done it sooner, before…well, before it went too far."

"I was wrong," he said. "I based it on my own experience. It was a different situation, and my wife and I were just kids. You're nothing like her. Once committed to somebody, you wouldn't let anything scare you off. Tanner's the same way. That's why I can't understand any of this."

She had no answer for him. He was right about her. But although she'd committed her heart to Tanner when she fell in love with him, it was best for both of them if she went on with her life and he went on with his. In time it would only hurt both of them more if she returned.

"I'm sorry, Dusty." Her voice wavered, but she hoped he realized things couldn't be any other way.

Shawn stood and faced her. "You're as stubborn as Uncle Tanner. I never thought you were a coward."

While she absorbed the blow his words had dealt, he glared at her. She was trying to think of something—anything—to say that would help him understand, if only a little.

Her breath caught when she heard Tanner's voice in the background on the phone—the voice that had haunted her, waking and sleeping, for three months.

"He's at Jules's place," she heard Dusty say.

"Give me the phone."

Jules gripped the receiver and attempted to calm her rampaging heart. What would he say? Would he tell her—

"Let me talk to Shawnee, Jules."

Opening her mouth to answer, she shook her head, unable to say anything to him, and held the phone out to Shawn. "It's Tanner."

He took it from her, but shot her a look meant to wound. "Uncle Tanner—" His frown deepened. "I just wanted to—" The determination in his eyes dimmed as he listened. "Yeah. Okay. But don't you want to talk to..."

Frightened at the thought of talking to Tanner, Jules took a step back. She couldn't risk her heart again, but even more, she couldn't bear to see him hurt again, not in a rodeo and especially not by her.

"All right. I'll meet him outside in ten minutes," Shawn said after taking a look at his watch. Replacing the phone in the cradle, he turned to Jules. "I guess I'll head out. A friend of Dusty's who lives here in Wichita is going to ride home with me, then go visit family in Oklahoma City."

The look of defeat and disappointment nearly broke down her defenses, but she refused to give in. It seemed everyone wanted her at the Rocking O. Everyone but Tanner. But then, even if he'd asked her to come back, she couldn't. Not as long as he continued to ride broncs. "I'm sorry, Shawn. I wish things were different."

Sad, blue-gray eyes looked into hers. "Me, too."

Speech was beyond her, so she merely nodded.

He reached into his back pocket and pulled out a folded, wrinkled envelope. "I found this in the trash."

Jules took it from him and stared at her name and address on the front, written in a bold, strong hand. Tears clogged her throat.

Shawn leaned forward and kissed her cheek. "I'm gonna miss you."

Choking back a sob, Jules nodded again. Not only had she fallen in love with Tanner, she loved his family. Shawn would never know how much she'd miss him, too.

With a wistful smile, Shawn turned to leave. The quiet click of the door closing behind him echoed in the room.

Jules stared at the door. She wished with all her heart that she could have asked him to take her back to the Rocking O with him. If she had, maybe... Shaking her head, she closed her mind off to the possibilities. Even if she thought she could get used to Tanner's career, one thing stopped her. Tanner had his pride. He might not want her, no matter how many others thought he did.

Her gaze fell on the envelope Shawn had given her. With fingers that trembled, she opened it and pulled open a single sheet of paper.

> Darlin—
> There's a plane ticket to Las Vegas waiting for you at the airport and a pass at the hotel to get into Finals.
> Please.
> Tanner

WITH LESS THAN three hours to go before his first ride in National Finals Rodeo, Tanner wandered through the lobby of the MGM Grand feeling lower than he had since his accident. They'd all been worried a few weeks earlier when Shawn had taken off in the ranch pickup. Certain he was somehow to blame for Shawn's disappearance, Tanner had been ready to call the authorities. At least it had taken his mind off Jules. Until he'd walked in to find that Shawn had gone to her place. Dumb kid. He'd only wanted to help, but it had been the last thing Tanner needed. He hadn't been able to talk to her. He should have, but there was nothing he could say to change her mind. She couldn't accept that he would continue competing, and he wouldn't give up his dream of riding for the championship. But somehow, without the woman he loved, it didn't seem nearly as important as it once had. A part of him had died when she walked out of that hospital room.

He'd always thought he understood what being lonely meant. As a small boy, he'd lost his mother to the lure of rodeo excitement. He'd gotten through it, grown to be a teenager and lost his father. Three years later, his brother had vanished. But none of it had been like the loneliness he felt now without Jules.

He approached the front desk to leave a message for Rowdy and heard Dusty hail him. Finishing his business, Tanner joined his friend.

Dusty gave him a friendly slap on the back. "You look mighty grim. Let me buy you a drink."

"Thanks," he answered, shaking his head, "but I'll pass."

Taking his arm, Dusty steered Tanner across the lobby to one of the hotel bars. "Then come keep me company. Although I don't know if I want to look at your sour face."

"That's fine," Tanner said, starting to pull away. He didn't have the energy to keep up appearances. He'd done enough of that with his family.

"No, no." Dusty swung him back around and they stepped into the low-lit room. "There's somebody I want you to meet."

Just what he didn't need, but Dusty could be as belligerent as a stuck cow at times. Tanner gave a shrug and reluctantly followed. One drink wouldn't matter. And after he'd finished his ride, he'd spend the night in his room, maybe with a bottle. Feeling generous, he decided Dusty could join him. Both of them had been badly burned in the past.

As they moved away from the doorway, the light grew dimmer. Dusty led him toward a dark corner, and Tanner grew suspicious. "Where's this person you want me to meet?"

"Just over here."

At a corner table, Tanner caught a glimpse of a female figure. "No, thanks," he said, stopping in his tracks.

"Aw, come on, cowboy. It'll do you good." Dusty chuckled as he propelled him toward the table. "There's a pretty little lady over here who's been dying to meet a real champion bronc rider."

Tanner didn't want to meet any woman, but he knew Dusty too well to try to back out of it. They walked closer, and Tanner could see her. He stopped again, this time unable to move.

Head down, the figure at the table might have been unrecognizable except for the black hat on a head of long, blond hair, and skin that glowed like alabaster, even in the darkness.

His mouth went dry and his mind went blank. He knew those hands, too, clasped in front of her on the table. They'd caressed his face, loving and tender, and stroked him in the midst of lovemaking.

With a nudge from Dusty, Tanner moved, putting one foot in front of the other, and his gaze never left the crown of that black hat and the hammered silver band around the base of the crown. His heart cried out for release, but he refused it. He would face the pain seeing her again might cause. There was always the chance his mind was playing tricks on him. He'd lost count over the past three months how many times he'd thought he'd seen her, only to realize it wasn't her.

Before he reached the table, she lifted her head. His heart stopped in midbeat, then kicked into overdrive, thundering in his chest.

*Jules.*

Green eyes, cool as a mountain forest, raised to meet

his and snagged his soul. A soft smile slid across her kissing-perfect lips before it sputtered.

Dusty prodded Tanner's immobile body forward to the table and leaned down between them. "I'll leave you two alone," he said with a knowing glance at each of them.

Tanner gripped the back of the chair in front of him like a lifeline, unable to stop staring at her. Three months had done things to her he'd never imagined possible. When he'd seen her last, in his hospital room, she'd been worn-out. But it didn't compare to the exhaustion he saw now, even in the dark corner. It cut him deeply to think he might have caused it. If he'd talked to her, tried to explain how he felt about everything, maybe neither of them would have gone through what they had. From the look of her, he was certain her life hadn't been all roses, any more than his had. If he'd only told her how he felt about her. But he never had. He'd been too focused on getting to National Finals.

But she was here. Right here in front of him. It meant something. And he knew he had to work fast before she vanished again.

His wits scattered to the other three corners of the room, leaving him with no thoughts, until the memory of the first night they met drifted into his mind. Forcing himself to move, he touched the brim of his hat, his arm feeling like an anvil. He pried his tongue from the roof of his mouth to speak the only words he could think of.

"Evening, darlin'." They came out sounding as rough as old barn wood.

A smile flitted across her face, and she inclined her head the merest inch. "Mr. O'Brien."

His legs wobbled beneath him like a newborn colt's, and he quickly pulled the chair out and sat on it. Words tumbled into his mind, colliding, but he couldn't speak.

She looked down and then back up again. "I'm sorry," she murmured.

Puzzled by an apology he couldn't comprehend, he impulsively reached out and took her hand in his, gaining courage and strength from her touch. "For what?"

Her eyes closed and she shook her head. "Everything." Opening them again, she looked away. "We're just so different."

Courage grew with determination. "That's what makes us special," he told her. "We complement each other. I know what you give to me. I hope I give you something in return." He watched her throat work, and the simple show of emotion gave him more courage. "You've filled places in my life I never knew existed, darlin'. When you're not around, I can't breathe."

"When you...when that bronc stepped on you, I thought I'd lost you." She looked at him, her eyes brimming with tears. "It was too much, Tanner. I couldn't do it any more. My accident and your dad..."

He squeezed her hand. "It's not the same, darlin'. My dad was...well, he was a different man, a troubled man. Do you think I'm crazy enough to go out there in that arena and do what I do if I didn't know that?"

"No." Her lips trembled.

"I should be the one apologizing for not taking the time to explain things to you. I expected you to understand everything about rodeo. I take all the blame for it, darlin'. Can you forgive me?"

"Only if you can forgive me. I let my fear rule my life, all my decisions. But you've helped me learn an important lesson."

"What's that, darlin'?"

Her smile was soft and gentle, touching his heart. "I learned that caution is only good when used wisely. I didn't do that. I ran away from the one thing that made me happy because I was too cautious and wasn't willing to take a risk, and I was afraid of the risks *you* took."

"Life is full of risks, no matter who you are or what you do."

"I understand that now."

"I need you, Jules. Will you stay with me?"

When she didn't answer immediately, panic gripped him, and he knew he needed to say the things he'd left unsaid before. "Nothing is as important to me as you, darlin'. Not bareback bronc riding. Not the buckles I've spent my life working for. We can leave here right now, darlin', and I'll never—"

"You have a rodeo. An important one."

"You're more important."

"No, Tanner," she said, her smile returning. "My love for you is stronger than my fear. I won't let you quit. Not now. Not when you've come so far."

"It doesn't matter, darlin'. You do."

"It *does* matter, Tanner. It matters to me."

Tanner could hardly believe it. He knew how much courage it took for her to say that. "All right, but you don't have to go to the arena if you don't want to. I can understand that. And you need to understand that I'm not going to ride broncs forever. Another year, maybe two. If I don't make it to the top, I'll know it isn't meant to be. But I have to try. I want you with me. I need you with me."

"I need you, too," she answered, her voice soft and husky. "I'll stay with you, and I'll watch every ride until you don't need me anymore."

Emotions rolled over him, flooding his heart and mind. The urge to laugh and cry and shout to the heavens filled him. But he hadn't finished.

"Nope. That's not good enough."

Her eyes widened, and she tried to pull away, but he held tight to her hand. "You'll have to marry me, darlin'. It's the only way I can be sure it'll be forever."

"Tanner O'Brien!" she gasped, and then her smile lit the dark corner. "Is this a proposal?"

Aching to hold her, he stood and drew her to her feet. Wrapping her in his arms, he gazed into the green depths of her eyes. "I love you, Jules Vandeveer. Will you marry me?"

Her eyes danced with love. "Yes, darlin'."

# *Epilogue*

"Thank you all for coming today to honor this year's National Finals Rodeo bareback riding champion!" Mayor Shinley's voice filled the Desperation, Oklahoma, football field and brought the crowd in the stands to its feet. When they quieted, he continued, "After competing professionally for sixteen years, he competed for the first time last year in the NFR and came home with fourth place. This year he returned to the NFR, took it by storm and gave those of us who watched on television and those who were there a thrill a minute. Please show how proud we are of Desperation's own Tanner O'Brien!"

Jules's heart filled with pride, and she leaned down to say, "Pay attention now, Wyoming. Your daddy's out there with the mayor."

The tiny bundle in her arms gurgled back at her, oblivious to the noise and lights. His bright blue eyes brought tears of joy to Jules's own.

Jules's parents, in the row behind her, added their own cheers to those of the townspeople. Sheila Vandeveer leaned over, still applauding. "We're just so happy for both of you, honey," she said.

"He's an exceptional athlete and a great young man," Schulyer Vandeveer, her father, added.

"I'm so glad you could be here today," Jules told them. "It means so much to both of us."

Rowdy leaned across Shawn, sitting next to her. "Jules, he's getting ready to say something."

She struggled to stand with the others. Bridey, on her other side, reached for the baby. "Here, give him to me. You can't see, and you're going to miss it all."

Jules handed her the three-month-old Wyoming and stood. "We're in the front row," she said, laughing. "You just want an excuse to hold him."

Rowdy leaned over to frown at all of them. "Hush, he's going to say something. And give me that boy." He took Wyoming from Bridey, cooing at him, and then glared at the two women. "I swear, you women coddle this little fella too much." He turned the baby in his arms to face the arena. "Now you watch, Wyoming. Don't pay any attention to your mama and Aunt Bridey."

Laughing, Jules turned to focus her attention on her husband, who now stood with the mayor.

But it was the mayor who stepped up to the microphone, while Tanner stood next to him on the raised platform at the fifty-yard line, looking only a little uncomfortable.

"Seeing as how we've never had a National Finals Rodeo champion here in Desperation, the city council put their heads together and decided to do something never done before." He turned to take something from Councilman Mike Stacy and then turned back again. "Tanner O'Brien, the City of Desperation, Oklahoma, would like to present you with the first key to the city."

While the crowd cheered, Tanner accepted the large gold key, turning it over lovingly in his hands. The crowd quieted when he stepped up to the microphone, and when he cleared his throat, the sound amplified through the speaker system. Ducking his head, he chuckled. "I'm not used to public speaking. I'm more at home on the back of a bronc or rounding up cattle on the Rocking O."

Grinning, he looked down at the key in his hands and shook his head. "It's been a big year for me. Last year I went to Las Vegas for the first time, a single cowboy, footloose and fancy-free. Well, not exactly. A very special lady joined me there, and when I left, not only did I take home fourth place, but a new wife. Now that's something to brag about.

"This year, I went with my darlin' wife, our three-month-old son and high hopes of doing better."

The crowd applauded the announcement, and Shawn grinned at Jules. "Let's see, nine months and three months. Seems to me he left Vegas last year with more than a new wife."

"Shawnee O'Brien!" Jules scolded. "Watch it, young man, or when you graduate, you'll be working your way through college on the back of a bucking bronc."

His grin widened. "Sounds good to me."

She shushed him, and when the crowd grew quiet again, Tanner continued, "This year, my dream came true, and now I'd like to fulfill my wife's dream. My dad told me once that a smart man steps down while he's ridin' high. And since I like to think I'm a smart man, this has been my last rodeo. I've decided to retire."

Stunned, Jules couldn't move. The crowd around her let out a collective groan, but her heart soared. She'd expected him to continue riding. They'd even discussed what it would be like when Wyoming was old enough to walk. Nothing Tanner could have said would have meant more to her.

"Thank you, all," Tanner finished. With his gaze on his wife, he walked up to the front of the platform, removed his hat and sailed it through the air in her direction.

Jules watched the hat float until it hit the railing in front of her and fell at her feet. Bending over, she picked it up, blinded by the tears in her eyes.

"My hat, darlin'."

She looked down into a pair of the bluest eyes she'd ever seen. Leaning over the railing, she placed the hat on Tanner's head. Caring little for the people around them, she pulled him to her and wrapped her arms around his neck, rewarding him with a long kiss. "Thank you, Tanner," she whispered.

He hauled her over the railing and into his arms. "Anytime, darlin'."

Cheers and whistles rocked the arena, but she never noticed. The only thing that mattered was the man holding her. "That was some surprise."

Tanner pushed his hat back on his head and looked down at her. "No more bronc riding, darlin'," he told her, a twinkle in his eye. "At least not for me. We will have to get you used to Shawn's, though."

Jules groaned, but had to smile at how far they'd come. "And here I thought my worries were all taken care of."

"Not quite," he said, chuckling. "And then, of course, there's Wyoming. We'll start him out on sheep in a year or two, then go on to calves and ponies. How does that sound?"

She laughed and kissed him again. "I'll deal with it then. Maybe I'll learn to like it, after all." She lost herself in the depths of his clear blue eyes. "But I'll always love you."

"That's all that matters, darlin'."

\* \* \* \* \*

RICK'S APPOINTMENT with his attorney early Wednesday morning went only moderately better than his meeting with social services the day before. The prognosis wasn't great—but at least his attorney was going to file a motion for DNA testing. Just so Rick could petition to see the child...his sister's baby. The sister he didn't know he had until it was too late.

The rest of what his attorney said had been downhill from there.

Cell phone in hand before he'd even reached his Nitro, Rick punched in the speed dial number he'd programmed the day before.

Maybe foster parent Sue Bookman hadn't received his message. Or had lost his number. Maybe she didn't want to talk to him. At this point he didn't much care what she wanted.

"Hello?" She answered before the first ring was complete. And sounded breathless.

Young and breathless.

"Ms. Bookman?"

"Yes. This is Rick Kraynick, right?"

"Yes, ma'am."

"I recognized your number on caller ID," she said,

her voice uneven, as though she was still engaged in whatever physical activity had her so breathless to begin with. "I'm sorry I didn't get back to you. I've been a little...distracted."

The words came in more disjointed spurts. Was she jogging?

"No problem," he said, when, in fact, he'd spent the better part of the night before watching his phone. And fretting. "Did I get you at a bad time?"

"No worse than usual," she said, adding, "better than some. So, how can I help?"

God, if only this could be so easy. He'd ask. She'd help. And life could go well. At least for one little person in his family.

It would be a first.

"Mr. Kraynick?"

"Yes. Sorry. I was...are you sure there isn't a better time to call?"

"I'm bouncing a baby, Mr. Kraynick. It's what I do."

"Is it Carrie?" he asked quickly, his pulse racing.

"How do you know Carrie?" She sounded defensive, which wouldn't do him any good.

"I'm her uncle," he explained, "her mother's—Christy's—older brother, and I know you have her."

"I can neither confirm nor deny your allegations, Mr. Kraynick. Please call social services." She rattled off the number.

"Wait!" he said, unable to hide his urgency. "Please," he said more calmly. "Just hear me out."

"How did you find me?"

"A friend of Christy's."

"I'm sorry I can't help you, Mr. Kraynick," she said softly. "This conversation is over."

"I grew up in foster care," he said, as though that gave him some special privilege. Some insider's edge.

"Then you know you shouldn't be calling me at all."

"Yes… But Carrie is my niece," he said. "I need to see her. To know that she's okay."

"You'll have to go through social services to arrange that."

"I'm sure you know it's not as easy as it sounds. I'm a single man with no real ties and I've no intention of petitioning for custody. They aren't real eager to give me the time of day. I never even knew Carrie's mother. For all intents and purposes, our mother didn't raise either one of us. All I have going for me is half a set of genes. My lawyer's on it, but it could be weeks— months—before this is sorted out. Carrie could be adopted by then. Which would be fine, great for her, but then I'd have lost my chance. I don't want to take her. I won't hurt her. I just have to see her."

"I'm sorry, Mr. Kraynick, but…"

\* \* \* \* \*

*Find out if Rick Kraynick will ever
have a chance to meet his niece.
Look for A DAUGHTER'S TRUST
by Tara Taylor Quinn,
available in September 2009.*

We'll be spotlighting a different series
every month throughout 2009
to celebrate our 60th anniversary.

**Look for Harlequin® Superromance®
in September!**

*Celebrate with
The Diamond Legacy
miniseries!*

Follow the stories of four cousins as they come to terms
with the complications of love and what it means to
be a family. Discover with them the sixty-year-old secret
that rocks not one but two families.

A DAUGHTER'S TRUST by *Tara Taylor Quinn*
**September**

FOR THE LOVE OF FAMILY by *Kathleen O'Brien*
**October**

LIKE FATHER, LIKE SON by *Karina Bliss*
**November**

A MOTHER'S SECRET by *Janice Kay Johnson*
**December**

**Available wherever books are sold.**

# You're invited to join our Tell Harlequin Reader Panel!

By joining our new reader panel you will:

- Receive Harlequin® books—they are FREE and yours to keep with no obligation to purchase anything!
- Participate in fun online surveys
- Exchange opinions and ideas with women just like you
- Have a say in our new book ideas and help us publish the best in women's fiction

*In addition, you will have a chance to win great prizes and receive special gifts!*
*See Web site for details. Some conditions apply.*
*Space is limited.*

To join, visit us at
# www.TellHarlequin.com.

# REQUEST YOUR FREE BOOKS!
## 2 FREE NOVELS PLUS 2
# FREE GIFTS!

### Love, Home & Happiness!

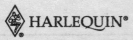

HARLEQUIN®

*American ★ Romance*®

# The Ranger's Secret
## REBECCA WINTERS

When Yosemite Park ranger Chase Jarvis rescues
an injured passenger from a downed helicopter,
he is stunned to discover it's the woman he
once loved. But Chase is no longer the man
Annie Bower knew. Will she forgive him for
the secret he's been keeping for ten long years?
And will he forgive Annie for her own secret—
the daughter Chase didn't know he had…?

*Available September
wherever books are sold.*

## "LOVE, HOME & HAPPINESS"

www.eHarlequin.com

HAR75279

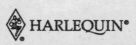

# COMING NEXT MONTH
## Available September 8, 2009

**#1273 DOCTOR DADDY by Jacqueline Diamond**
*Men Made in America*
Dr. Jane McKay wants a child more than anything, but her dreams
of parenthood don't include the sexy, maddening doctor next door.
Luke Van Dam is *not* ready to settle down. Yet the gorgeous babe magnet
seems to attract *babies*, too—he's just become guardian of an infant girl.
Is Luke the right man to share Jane's dream after all?

**#1274 ONCE A COP by Lisa Childs**
*Citizen's Police Academy*
Roberta "Robbie" Meyers wants a promotion out of the Lakewood P.D. vice
squad so she can spend more time with her daughter. Holden Thomas sees only a
woman with a job that's too dangerous for a mother. So the bachelor guardian
strikes Robbie off his list of mommy candidates for the little girl under his care.
Too bad he can't resist the attractive cop's charms!

**#1275 THE RANGER'S SECRET by Rebecca Winters**
When Chase Jarvis rescues an injured passenger from a downed helicopter, the
Yosemite ranger is stunned to discover it's the woman he once loved. But he is
no longer the man Annie Bower knew. Will she forgive him for the secret he's
been keeping for ten long years? And will he forgive Annie her own secret—the
daughter Chase didn't know he had...?

**#1276 A WEDDING FOR BABY by Laura Marie Altom**
*Baby Boom*
Gabby Craig's pregnancy is a dream come true. Too bad the father is an
unreliable, no-good charmer who's left town. And when his brother, Dane, steps
in to help, Gabby can't help relying on the handsome, *responsible* judge. But
how can she be falling for the brother of her baby's daddy?

www.eHarlequin.com

HARCNMBPA0809